The AI ERA & Humanities 2024

C.W. Fortney

Published by C.W. Fortney, 2024.

THE AI ERA & HUMANITIES 2024

First edition. February 16, 2024.

ISBN: 979-8223650966

Written by C.W. Fortney.

Table of Contents

The AI ERA & Humanities 2024 1

Career Navigation 6

The Convergence of The AI Era and Humanities 9

Overcome AI Inertia 11

The Intersection of Technology and Humanities 13

Bridging the human heart with Artificial Superintelligence (ASI) 53

Humans with ethics and good morals 54

Critical role of ethics and morals 55

The New Frontier is Here ASI & Humanities 2024 56

Let's Get Started with important knowledge!

The AI era brings about numerous benefits, challenges, and potential risks. Let's explore the "good," the "bad," and the "ugly" aspects of the AI era:

The Good:

Advancements in Technology: AI has led to significant advancements in various fields, including healthcare, finance, transportation, and entertainment. It has the potential to improve efficiency, productivity, and innovation across industries.

Automation of Repetitive Tasks: AI technologies enable the automation of repetitive and mundane tasks, freeing up human workers to focus on more creative, strategic, and high-value activities. This can lead to increased productivity and job satisfaction.

Enhanced Decision-Making: AI algorithms can analyze large volumes of data and identify patterns, trends, and insights that may not be apparent to human analysts. This can help businesses make more informed decisions, optimize processes, and improve outcomes.

Personalized Experiences: AI-powered personalization allows companies to deliver tailored experiences, recommendations, and services to individual users based on their preferences, behaviors, and interests. This can enhance customer satisfaction, engagement, and loyalty.

Addressing Societal Challenges: AI has the potential to address complex societal challenges, such as healthcare disparities, environmental sustainability, and economic inequality. By leveraging AI technologies, researchers and policymakers can develop innovative solutions to pressing global issues.

The Bad:

Job Displacement: The automation of jobs and tasks by AI technologies can lead to job displacement, particularly for workers in industries that rely heavily on manual labor or routine tasks. This can contribute to unemployment, income inequality, and economic instability.

Bias and Discrimination: AI systems may exhibit bias or discrimination based on the data they are trained on, leading to unfair or discriminatory outcomes, particularly for marginalized or underrepresented groups. Addressing bias in AI algorithms is a critical challenge that requires careful attention and mitigation strategies.

Privacy Concerns: The widespread adoption of AI technologies raises concerns about data privacy and security. AI systems often rely on large amounts of personal data to train and operate, raising questions about data ownership, consent, and protection against misuse or unauthorized access.

Ethical Dilemmas: AI introduces complex ethical dilemmas, such as the use of autonomous weapons, algorithmic decision-making in critical domains like healthcare and criminal justice, and the potential for AI to exacerbate social inequalities. Balancing innovation with ethical considerations is essential to ensure that AI technologies benefit society as a whole.

Technological Dependence: Society's increasing reliance on AI technologies raises concerns about technological dependence and vulnerability to system failures, cyberattacks, or manipulation. Ensuring the resilience and robustness of AI systems is essential to mitigate risks and maintain trust in the technology.

The Ugly:

Malicious Use of AI: The proliferation of AI technologies opens the door to malicious actors who may exploit AI for nefarious purposes, such as spreading disinformation, conducting cyberattacks, or developing autonomous weapons. Addressing the potential misuse of AI requires robust cybersecurity measures, regulatory frameworks, and international cooperation.

Unintended Consequences: The complexity and unpredictability of AI systems can lead to unintended consequences or unforeseen outcomes, including unintended biases, algorithmic errors, or unintended behaviors. Proactive risk assessment and monitoring are essential to identify and mitigate potential risks before they escalate.

Job Polarization: While AI may create new job opportunities in emerging fields such as data science, machine learning, and AI development, it may also exacerbate job polarization by creating a divide between high-skilled, high-paying jobs and low-skilled, low-paying jobs. Addressing skill gaps and promoting lifelong learning is essential to ensure that workers can adapt to the changing labor market.

Loss of Human Connection: The increasing automation and digitization driven by AI technologies may lead to a loss of human connection and empathy, particularly in industries that rely heavily on human interaction, such as healthcare, education, and customer service. Balancing technological efficiency with human-centered design is essential to preserve human dignity and well-being.

Existential Risks: Some experts warn of existential risks associated with the development of advanced AI systems, including the potential for superintelligent AI to surpass human intelligence and pose existential threats to humanity. Addressing these risks requires careful consideration of long-term consequences, ethical principles, and international cooperation to ensure the responsible development and deployment of AI technologies.

In summary, the AI era presents both opportunities and challenges for society, ranging from advancements in technology and improved decision-making to job displacement, bias, and ethical dilemmas. It is essential to address these issues proactively through collaboration, regulation, and responsible innovation to harness the benefits of AI while minimizing its potential risks and pitfalls.

In 2024, the intersection of humanities and AI is likely to continue to evolve and shape various aspects of society, culture, and education. Here are some potential developments and trends in the field of humanities with AI:

AI-Assisted Research: AI tools and algorithms can assist humanities scholars in conducting research, analyzing vast amounts of data, and generating insights across diverse disciplines such as history, literature, philosophy, and cultural studies. Natural language processing (NLP) techniques, sentiment analysis, and topic modeling can facilitate text analysis and interpretation, helping researchers uncover patterns, trends, and connections within large datasets of textual and multimedia sources.

Digital Humanities: Digital humanities, which combine computational methods with traditional humanities disciplines, are likely to see continued growth and innovation with the integration of AI technologies. Digital archives, digital storytelling platforms, and immersive experiences enabled by AI-driven natural language generation and virtual reality (VR) can enhance the accessibility and engagement of humanities scholarship and cultural heritage.

AI-Generated Art and Creativity: AI algorithms, such as generative adversarial networks (GANs) and deep learning models, are increasingly being used to generate art, music, literature, and other creative works. While debates around the authenticity and originality of AI-generated content persist, these technologies offer new avenues for exploration and experimentation in artistic expression, collaborative creativity, and the blurring of boundaries between human and machine creativity.

Ethical and Social Implications: The integration of AI in humanities research and cultural production raises important ethical and social considerations, including questions about algorithmic bias, data privacy, intellectual property rights, and the impact of automation on labor and creativity. Scholars in the humanities are likely to continue to explore these issues through interdisciplinary collaboration, critical reflection, and public engagement to ensure responsible and equitable use of AI technologies.

Education and Pedagogy: AI-driven personalized learning platforms, virtual tutors, and educational games can enhance humanities education by providing adaptive learning experiences, interactive simulations, and personalized feedback tailored to individual learners' needs and preferences. AI technologies can also facilitate the creation of digital learning resources, multimedia presentations, and collaborative projects that engage students in active learning and critical thinking across diverse humanities disciplines.

Overall, the integration of AI in the humanities offers exciting opportunities for innovation, discovery, and collaboration while raising important questions about the future of human creativity, knowledge production, and societal values. By embracing interdisciplinary approaches and ethical frameworks, scholars, educators, and creators can harness the transformative potential of AI to advance humanistic inquiry and enrich our understanding of the human experience.

I can extrapolate some potential ways in which AI might continue to impact society in 2024 based on existing trends:

Increased Automation: AI is likely continuing to automate various tasks across industries, leading to efficiency improvements and cost savings. This could result in job displacement in some sectors while creating opportunities for new types of jobs that require human-AI collaboration.

Enhanced Healthcare: AI-driven technologies could be revolutionizing healthcare by improving diagnostics, personalized treatment plans, and drug discovery. AI algorithms might be helping doctors make more accurate diagnoses and providing better insights from medical data.

Smarter Cities: AI-powered systems could be optimizing city infrastructure, leading to smarter transportation systems, energy management, and waste reduction. This might result in more sustainable and livable urban environments.

Personalized Experiences: AI-driven recommendation systems are likely providing increasingly personalized experiences in fields such as entertainment, e-commerce, and content consumption. This could lead to more targeted advertising and tailored services.

Ethical and Regulatory Challenges: As AI becomes more integrated into society, there may be increasing concerns about privacy, bias, and accountability. Governments and organizations may need to implement regulations and guidelines to ensure responsible AI development and deployment.

Education and Upskilling: With the rise of automation, there may be a greater emphasis on education and upskilling programs to prepare the workforce for jobs that require human creativity, empathy, and critical thinking skills—areas where AI currently struggles to replicate human capabilities.

AI in Governance: Governments might be using AI to improve decision-making processes, optimize resource allocation, and enhance public services. However, there could also be debates around the ethical implications of using AI in governance and policymaking.

Cybersecurity Challenges: With the increasing adoption of AI, there could be growing concerns about AI-driven cyber threats and the need for robust cybersecurity measures to protect sensitive data and critical infrastructure.

These are just a few potential ways in which AI could continue to shape society in 2024. The actual impact will depend on various factors, including technological advancements, regulatory frameworks, and societal attitudes towards AI

Humans play a crucial role in helping AI

systems learn, improve, and perform effectively. Here are several ways in which humans can contribute to the development and enhancement of AI:

Data Annotation and Labeling: Humans provide annotated data sets that serve as training examples for machine learning algorithms. This involves labeling images, text, audio, or video data with relevant tags or annotations to help AI systems learn to recognize patterns and make accurate predictions.

Feedback and Correction: Humans provide feedback to AI systems to correct errors, refine predictions, and improve performance. This may involve correcting misclassified data points, providing ratings or reviews, or flagging inaccuracies in AI-generated outputs.

Training and Supervision: Humans train and supervise AI systems during the learning process to ensure they adhere to desired behaviors and objectives. This includes providing guidance, setting objectives, and monitoring progress to ensure that AI systems learn effectively and align with human expectations.

Curating Training Data: Humans curate training data sets to ensure they are representative, diverse, and unbiased. This involves selecting relevant data samples, filtering out irrelevant or noisy data, and addressing biases or imbalances in the data to improve the robustness and fairness of AI models.

Interpreting and Explaining Outputs: Humans interpret and explain AI-generated outputs to make them understandable and actionable. This includes providing context, interpreting model predictions, and explaining the rationale behind AI-driven recommendations or decisions to end-users.

Domain Expertise and Knowledge Integration: Humans contribute domain expertise and specialized knowledge to AI systems to enhance their understanding and problem-solving capabilities in specific domains. This involves integrating human insights, rules, and constraints into AI models to improve their performance and relevance in real-world applications.

Continuous Improvement and Iterative Refinement: Humans engage in continuous improvement and iterative refinement of AI systems to address performance gaps, adapt to changing circumstances, and incorporate new insights and feedback. This involves monitoring performance metrics, conducting experiments, and iterating on AI algorithms and models to optimize outcomes over time.

Ensuring Ethical and Responsible AI: Humans play a critical role in ensuring that AI systems adhere to ethical principles, legal regulations, and societal norms. This includes evaluating the ethical implications of AI applications, mitigating biases and discrimination, and designing AI systems that prioritize human well-being and societal values.

Overall, humans contribute to AI development and deployment by providing expertise, guidance, and feedback throughout the AI lifecycle, from data collection and model training to deployment and evaluation. By fostering collaboration between humans and AI systems, we can harness the full potential of AI to address complex challenges and enhance human capabilities in diverse domains.

Driving Force of AIThe driving force behind **Artificial Intelligence (AI)** is multifaceted and fueled by several key factors:

Big Data:

The exponential growth of data provides AI systems with ample training material.

AI algorithms learn from vast datasets[1]

Processing Power:

Advances in computing hardware, including GPUs and specialized AI chips, accelerate AI model training.

High-performance computing allows complex neural networks to process data[2]

---

1. https://www.bing.com/

aclick?ld=e8BU6eeFyVGtAcpC6Mug5N5DVUCUwp4AewbCWBanYNAS0sbVabQ3BIENeBCt8GCBlnq2Ntf7xtUdSVxpvvm9cFjUv1CMaOFu98Kss8sp5Mlh

YDHeLVBU958LYT2Eht1LG6ZD8enSNYYqNTlkLvytXzCHb02IolSvsovOvuI5tAhWTMIqZi&u=aHR0cHMlM2ElMmYlMmZ3d3cuaHJibG9jay5jb20lMm

ZscCUyZnRheC1maWxpbmclMmYlM2ZvdHBwYXJ0bmVyaWQlM2Q5MDA5JTI2Y2FtcGFpZ25pZCUzZHBzX21jbV85MDA5XzcwMDRfZnkyNF9sb2ItZ

2N0XzEwNF9wMDFfYTA4XzcxNzAwMDAwMTE2ODYwMTQ1XzU4NzAwMDA4NjQ0MzM4MjkyX3RheCUyYnJldHVybiUyYmZpbGluZyUyNmdjbGlk

JTNkOGQzYmRmZGZjZjkyMTU5MzNiMmJiYTE5NTEwNzZjYmYlMjZnY2xzcmMlM2QzcC5kcyUyNm1zY2xraWQlM2Q4ZDNiZGZkZmNmOTIxNTkz

M2IyYmJhMTk1MTA3NmNiZg&rlid=8d3bdfdfcf9215933b2bba1951076cbf

2. https://www.bing.com/

aclick?ld=e8BU6eeFyVGtAcpC6Mug5N5DVUCUwp4AewbCWBanYNAS0sbVabQ3BIENeBCt8GCBlnq2Ntf7xtUdSVxpvvm9cFjUv1CMaOFu98Kss8sp5Mlh

YDHeLVBU958LYT2Eht1LG6ZD8enSNYYqNTlkLvytXzCHb02IolSvsovOvuI5tAhWTMIqZi&u=aHR0cHMlM2ElMmYlMmZ3d3cuaHJibG9jay5jb20lMm

ZscCUyZnRheC1maWxpbmclMmYlM2ZvdHBwYXJ0bmVyaWQlM2Q5MDA5JTI2Y2FtcGFpZ25pZCUzZHBzX21jbV85MDA5XzcwMDRfZnkyNF9sb2ItZ

2N0XzEwNF9wMDFfYTA4XzcxNzAwMDAwMTE2ODYwMTQ1XzU4NzAwMDA4NjQ0MzM4MjkyX3RheCUyYnJldHVybiUyYmZpbGluZyUyNmdjbGlk

Connected Globe:

Global connectivity facilitates data sharing, collaboration, and access to diverse information.

AI benefits from a networked world where insights can be drawn from various[3]

Open-Source Software:

Open-source AI frameworks (e.g., TensorFlow, PyTorch) democratize AI development.

Collaboration and community contributions drive innovation[4]

Improved Algorithms:

Researchers continually refine AI algorithms, enhancing their accuracy and efficiency.

Innovations in deep learning, reinforcement learning, and natural language[5]

Accelerating Returns:

As AI evolves, it accelerates its own progress.

Feedback loops lead to iterative improvements, creating a self-reinforcing cycle[6]

JTNkOGQzYmRmZGZjZjkyMTU5MzNiMmJiYTE5NTEwNzZjYmYlMjZnY2xzcmMlM2QzcC5kcyUyNm1zY2xraWQlM2Q4ZDNiZGZkZmNmOTIxNTkz
M2IyYmJhMTk1MTA3NmNiZg&rlid=8d3bdfdfcf9215933b2bba1951076cbf

3. https://www.bing.com/

aclick?ld=e8BU6eeFyVGtAcpC6Mug5N5DVUCUwp4AewbCWBanYNAS0sbVabQ3BIENeBCt8GCBlnq2Ntf7xtUdSVxpvvm9cFjUv1CMaOFu98Kss8sp5Mlh
YDHeLVBU958LYT2Eht1LG6ZD8enSNYYqNTlkLvytXzCHb02IolSvsovOvuI5tAhWTMIqZi&u=aHR0cHMlM2ElMmYlMmZ3d3cuaHJibG9jay5jb20lMm
ZscCUyZnRheC1maWxpbmclMmYlM2ZvdHBwYXJ0bmVyaWQlM2Q5MDA5JTI2Y2FtcGFpZ25pZCUzZHBzX21jbV85MDA5XzcwMDRfZnkyNF9sb2ItZItZ
2N0XzEwNF9wMDFfYTA4XzczcxNzAwMDAwMTE2ODYwMTQ1XzU4NzAwMDA4NjQ0MzM4MjkyX3RheCUyNjldHVybiUyYmZpbGluZyUyNmdjbGlk
JTNkOGQzYmRmZGZjZjkyMTU5MzNiMmJiYTE5NTEwNzZjYmYlMjZnY2xzcmMlM2QzcC5kcyUyNm1zY2xraWQlM2Q4ZDNiZGZkZmNmOTIxNTkz
M2IyYmJhMTk1MTA3NmNiZg&rlid=8d3bdfdfcf9215933b2bba1951076cbf

4. https://www.bing.com/

aclick?ld=e8BU6eeFyVGtAcpC6Mug5N5DVUCUwp4AewbCWBanYNAS0sbVabQ3BIENeBCt8GCBlnq2Ntf7xtUdSVxpvvm9cFjUv1CMaOFu98Kss8sp5Mlh
YDHeLVBU958LYT2Eht1LG6ZD8enSNYYqNTlkLvytXzCHb02IolSvsovOvuI5tAhWTMIqZi&u=aHR0cHMlM2ElMmYlMmZ3d3cuaHJibG9jay5jb20lMm
ZscCUyZnRheC1maWxpbmclMmYlM2ZvdHBwYXJ0bmVyaWQlM2Q5MDA5JTI2Y2FtcGFpZ25pZCUzZHBzX21jbV85MDA5XzcwMDRfZnkyNF9sb2ItZItZ
2N0XzEwNF9wMDFfYTA4XzczcxNzAwMDAwMTE2ODYwMTQ1XzU4NzAwMDA4NjQ0MzM4MjkyX3RheCUyNjldHVybiUyYmZpbGluZyUyNmdjbGlk
JTNkOGQzYmRmZGZjZjkyMTU5MzNiMmJiYTE5NTEwNzZjYmYlMjZnY2xzcmMlM2QzcC5kcyUyNm1zY2xraWQlM2Q4ZDNiZGZkZmNmOTIxNTkz
M2IyYmJhMTk1MTA3NmNiZg&rlid=8d3bdfdfcf9215933b2bba1951076cbf

5. https://www.bing.com/

aclick?ld=e8BU6eeFyVGtAcpC6Mug5N5DVUCUwp4AewbCWBanYNAS0sbVabQ3BIENeBCt8GCBlnq2Ntf7xtUdSVxpvvm9cFjUv1CMaOFu98Kss8sp5Mlh
YDHeLVBU958LYT2Eht1LG6ZD8enSNYYqNTlkLvytXzCHb02IolSvsovOvuI5tAhWTMIqZi&u=aHR0cHMlM2ElMmYlMmZ3d3cuaHJibG9jay5jb20lMm
ZscCUyZnRheC1maWxpbmclMmYlM2ZvdHBwYXJ0bmVyaWQlM2Q5MDA5JTI2Y2FtcGFpZ25pZCUzZHBzX21jbV85MDA5XzcwMDRfZnkyNF9sb2ItZItZ
2N0XzEwNF9wMDFfYTA4XzczcxNzAwMDAwMTE2ODYwMTQ1XzU4NzAwMDA4NjQ0MzM4MjkyX3RheCUyNjldHVybiUyYmZpbGluZyUyNmdjbGlk
JTNkOGQzYmRmZGZjZjkyMTU5MzNiMmJiYTE5NTEwNzZjYmYlMjZnY2xzcmMlM2QzcC5kcyUyNm1zY2xraWQlM2Q4ZDNiZGZkZmNmOTIxNTkz
M2IyYmJhMTk1MTA3NmNiZg&rlid=8d3bdfdfcf9215933b2bba1951076cbf

6. https://becominghuman.ai/why-the-ai-revolution-now-because-of-6-key-factors-7ee92e482d2

Career Navigation

in the age of AI, establishing a comprehensive system of career navigation is crucial to help individuals adapt to the rapidly evolving job market and technological landscape. Here's why such a system is necessary and how it could benefit people:

Adapting to Technological Changes: AI and automation are reshaping the labor market, leading to the emergence of new job roles and the obsolescence of others. A career navigation system can help individuals understand these changes and identify opportunities for upskilling, reskilling, or transitioning to new career paths.

Personalized Guidance: Different individuals have unique skills, interests, and career aspirations. A career navigation system can provide personalized guidance based on an individual's strengths, preferences, and goals, helping them make informed decisions about their career path.

Continuous Learning: Lifelong learning is becoming increasingly important in the age of AI, as individuals need to continuously update their skills and knowledge to remain competitive in the job market. A career navigation system can facilitate access to educational resources, training programs, and professional development opportunities tailored to individuals' needs and interests.

Promoting Career Mobility: In a dynamic and interconnected world, career mobility is essential for individuals to explore diverse opportunities and pursue fulfilling careers. A career navigation system can help individuals explore different career paths, industries, or geographical locations, facilitating career mobility and flexibility.

Supporting Career Transitions: As industries evolve and job roles change, individuals may need support transitioning between different careers or sectors. A career navigation system can provide guidance, resources, and support services to help individuals navigate career transitions smoothly and successfully.

Building Resilience: The future of work is characterized by uncertainty and rapid change. A career navigation system can help individuals build resilience by equipping them with the skills, knowledge, and resources needed to adapt to new challenges and seize emerging opportunities in the job market.

Overall, a system of career navigation is essential in the age of AI to empower individuals to navigate their career paths effectively, adapt to technological changes, and thrive in the evolving job market. By providing personalized guidance, promoting continuous learning, and supporting career mobility and transitions, such a system can help individuals build fulfilling and resilient careers in the digital age.

The quest to imbue artificial intelligence with moral capacity

In the AI era of 2024, the quest to imbue artificial intelligence with moral capacity has become increasingly vital. Here are some key considerations and approaches in this endeavor:

Ethical Frameworks: Engineers and ethicists are working on integrating ethical frameworks into AI systems, ensuring they operate within established moral guidelines. This involves encoding principles such as fairness, transparency, accountability, and respect for human rights into the design and operation of AI.

Value Alignment: Researchers are exploring methods to align AI systems' values with those of human society. This involves understanding human values and preferences and designing AI systems that respect and promote them.

Explainability and Transparency: AI systems must be transparent and explainable to users and stakeholders. This transparency helps build trust and allows humans to understand the reasoning behind AI decisions, which is crucial for ethical accountability.

Human-in-the-Loop Systems: Human oversight and intervention are essential for ensuring AI systems act morally. Human-in-the-loop systems empower humans to review and correct AI decisions, preventing harmful outcomes and reinforcing ethical behavior.

Continuous Learning and Adaptation: AI systems should be capable of learning and adapting their behavior based on feedback from their environment and human stakeholders. This enables them to evolve ethically over time and respond appropriately to changing circumstances.

Cross-Disciplinary Collaboration: Ethical AI development requires collaboration across diverse fields, including computer science, ethics, psychology, sociology, law, and philosophy. By bringing together experts from these disciplines, we can address the complex moral challenges posed by AI technology.

Regulatory Frameworks: Governments and international organizations are developing regulatory frameworks to govern the development and deployment of AI systems. These regulations aim to ensure AI technologies are developed and used in ways that are ethical, transparent, and aligned with societal values.

Ethical Education and Awareness: Educating AI developers, policymakers, and the general public about ethical considerations in AI is essential. This includes raising awareness about potential ethical pitfalls, promoting ethical literacy, and fostering a culture of responsible AI development and use.

By addressing these challenges and adopting these approaches, we can work towards ensuring that AI systems in the 2024 era possess the moral capacity necessary to contribute positively to society while minimizing potential harm.

Imbuing artificial intelligence (AI) with moral capacity is a complex and multifaceted challenge that involves addressing ethical, philosophical, technical, and societal considerations. While AI systems can be designed to adhere to ethical principles and guidelines, achieving true moral capacity in AI raises fundamental questions about consciousness, empathy, and moral agency. Here are some key considerations for imbuing AI with moral capacity:

Ethical Frameworks: Designing AI systems with ethical principles and values is essential for ensuring responsible and ethical behavior. Ethical frameworks, such as fairness, transparency, accountability, and privacy, can guide the development and deployment of AI technologies to minimize harm and promote human well-being.

Value Alignment: Aligning AI systems with human values and preferences requires understanding and incorporating diverse cultural, social, and ethical perspectives into the design process. Value alignment techniques, such as inverse reinforcement learning, value alignment algorithms, and preference elicitation, can help bridge the gap between AI behavior and human values.

Ethical Decision-Making: Implementing ethical decision-making capabilities in AI systems involves enabling machines to reason about moral dilemmas, make ethical judgments, and act in accordance with ethical principles. Ethical decision-making frameworks, such as deontological ethics, consequentialism, and virtue ethics, can inform the development of AI algorithms that prioritize ethical outcomes and considerations.

Explainability and Interpretability: Ensuring transparency and interpretability in AI systems is critical for understanding and justifying their decisions and actions. Explainable AI techniques, such as model interpretability, decision explanations, and transparency tools, can provide insights into how AI systems make moral judgments and recommendations.

Human Oversight and Control: Maintaining human oversight and control over AI systems is essential for accountability, oversight, and intervention in case of ethical violations or unintended consequences. Human-in-the-loop and human-on-the-loop approaches enable humans to monitor, evaluate, and intervene in AI decision-making processes to ensure alignment with ethical principles and values.

Continuous Learning and Adaptation: Building AI systems that can learn, adapt, and evolve their ethical behavior over time requires mechanisms for continuous learning, feedback, and adaptation. Reinforcement learning, evolutionary algorithms, and adaptive control techniques can enable AI systems to update their ethical models and policies based on new information and feedback from human stakeholders.

Ethical Governance and Regulation: Establishing governance mechanisms and regulatory frameworks for AI is essential for ensuring accountability, transparency, and compliance with ethical standards and legal requirements.

Ethical guidelines, codes of conduct, and regulatory frameworks can provide guidance and oversight for the development, deployment, and use of AI technologies in society.

While imbuing AI with moral capacity presents significant challenges, addressing these considerations can help foster responsible and ethical AI development and deployment that aligns with human values and aspirations. By integrating ethical principles, human oversight, and societal engagement into the design and governance of AI systems, we can work towards creating AI technologies that contribute positively to human well-being and societal progress.

The idea of imbuing **Artificial Intelligence (AI)** with moral capacity is a topic of ongoing research and debate. Compassionate AI is one such approach that aims to integrate ethics, empathy, and societal values into AI design and deployment.

Compassionate AI could help mitigate biases, enhance well-being, and foster stronger human-machine interactions However, the implementation of compassionate AI is not without its challenges. For instance, it is difficult to define and quantify compassion, and there is no consensus on how to integrate it into AI systems. Some researchers suggest that compassionate AI could be designed to be more than intelligent, intuitive, and compassionate, as it makes decisions that affect all of our lives. Others argue that AI should be designed to be transparent, accountable, and aligned with human values.

While the idea of compassionate AI is still in its infancy, it has the potential to shape the future of AI development and deployment.

The Convergence of The AI Era and Humanities

The convergence of the AI era and humanities represents an intriguing intersection where the capabilities of artificial intelligence intersect with the exploration of human culture, expression, and understanding. Here's how this meeting unfolds:

AI in Language and Literature: Natural Language Processing (NLP) and machine learning algorithms are applied to analyze literary texts, identify themes, track linguistic evolution, and even generate new content in the style of famous authors. These tools provide scholars with novel insights into literature, language, and the human condition.

Cultural Analysis and Social Sciences: AI enables the analysis of vast amounts of cultural data, including social media posts, historical records, and cultural artifacts. By applying machine learning algorithms, researchers can uncover patterns, trends, and cultural dynamics, shedding light on societal values, beliefs, and behaviors across different contexts and time periods.

Digital Humanities and Computational Methods: Digital humanities utilize computational techniques to explore and interpret cultural phenomena, historical events, and artistic expressions. From text mining and network analysis to GIS mapping and data visualization, AI-driven approaches offer new avenues for interdisciplinary research and collaboration in the humanities.

Artificial Creativity and Expressive Arts: AI systems are increasingly capable of generating creative outputs in various artistic domains, including music composition, visual arts, and storytelling. Collaborations between artists, programmers, and AI systems blur the boundaries between human and machine creativity, raising questions about authorship, originality, and aesthetic value.

Ethical and Philosophical Reflections: The rise of AI prompts profound ethical and philosophical inquiries about the nature of intelligence, consciousness, and human identity. Humanities scholars engage with these questions, exploring the ethical implications of AI technologies, their impact on society, and the ethical responsibilities of AI creators and users.

Digital Culture and Identity: AI-mediated interactions shape contemporary digital culture and influence how individuals perceive themselves and others online. Humanities perspectives provide critical insights into the construction of identity, community formation, and the mediation of human relationships in the context of AI-driven social platforms and virtual environments.

Education and Empowerment: Integrating AI tools and methodologies into humanities education empowers students to develop critical thinking skills, computational literacy, and digital fluency. By engaging with AI technologies, students gain a deeper understanding of humanistic inquiry and its relevance to contemporary challenges and opportunities.

The convergence of the AI era and humanities offers fertile ground for interdisciplinary exploration, fostering dialogue, innovation, and collaboration between AI researchers, technologists, and scholars in the humanities. By leveraging AI capabilities to deepen our understanding of human culture, creativity, and ethics, we can navigate the complexities of the AI-driven world while honoring the richness and diversity of human experience.

The interdisciplinary nature of AI and humanities

The interdisciplinary nature of AI and humanities refers to the intersection and collaboration between artificial intelligence (AI) technologies and the study of human culture, history, language, literature, philosophy, and the arts. This intersection offers rich opportunities for cross-disciplinary exploration, innovation, and collaboration. Here are some key aspects of the interdisciplinary nature of AI and humanities:

Technological Advancements in Humanities Research: AI technologies, such as natural language processing (NLP), machine learning, and computer vision, provide powerful tools for analyzing, interpreting, and preserving cultural artifacts, historical documents, and linguistic data. These technologies enable humanities scholars to uncover new insights, patterns, and trends in human culture and history.

Digital Humanities: Digital humanities is an interdisciplinary field that applies computational techniques to study and interpret cultural phenomena, historical events, and artistic expressions. By leveraging AI-driven approaches, such as text mining, network analysis, and data visualization, scholars can explore complex research questions and collaborate across disciplinary boundaries.

AI in Creative Expression: AI technologies are increasingly used in creative domains, such as art, music, literature, and design, where they can generate content, assist in the creative process, and inspire new forms of expression. Collaborations between artists, writers, and AI systems blur the boundaries between human and machine creativity, sparking new conversations about authorship, originality, and artistic innovation.

Ethical and Philosophical Inquiries: The rise of AI prompts profound ethical and philosophical inquiries about the nature of intelligence, consciousness, and human identity. Humanities scholars engage with these questions, exploring the ethical implications of AI technologies, their impact on society, and the ethical responsibilities of AI creators and users.

Education and Outreach: Integrating AI tools and methodologies into humanities education empowers students to develop critical thinking skills, computational literacy, and digital fluency. By engaging with AI technologies, students gain a deeper understanding of humanistic inquiry and its relevance to contemporary challenges and opportunities.

Cultural Heritage Preservation: Technology plays a crucial role in preserving and restoring cultural heritage sites, artworks, and artifacts. Techniques such as 3D scanning, photogrammetry, and remote sensing are used to create detailed digital replicas of cultural objects, which can be archived, studied, and shared globally.

Ethical and Social Implications: Humanistic perspectives contribute to discussions about the ethical and social implications of AI technology, including issues related to bias, fairness, transparency, accountability, and the impact of AI on society. By integrating humanistic insights into AI development and deployment, we can ensure that AI systems align with human values and respect human rights.

Overall, the interdisciplinary nature of AI and humanities fosters collaboration, innovation, and critical reflection, enriching our understanding of the human experience and shaping the responsible development and use of AI technology in society.

Overcome AI Inertia

Overcoming AI inertia involves addressing various challenges that hinder the adoption and advancement of artificial intelligence technologies. Here are some strategies to overcome AI inertia:

Education and Awareness: Increase education and awareness about AI among businesses, policymakers, and the general public. Providing training programs, workshops, and educational resources can help demystify AI and its potential benefits, encouraging more organizations to explore its applications.

Addressing Data Challenges: Data quality, accessibility, and privacy concerns are common barriers to AI adoption. Organizations should invest in data management strategies, data governance frameworks, and data privacy measures to ensure the availability of high-quality data for AI applications while maintaining compliance with regulations.

Building AI Talent: The shortage of skilled AI professionals is a significant challenge for many organizations. Investing in AI talent development through training programs, academic partnerships, and talent acquisition initiatives can help address this shortage and build internal expertise in AI technologies.

Developing Ethical Guidelines: Establish clear ethical guidelines and principles for the development and deployment of AI technologies. This includes addressing issues such as fairness, transparency, accountability, and bias mitigation to ensure that AI systems are developed and used responsibly.

Promoting Interdisciplinary Collaboration: Foster collaboration between AI researchers, domain experts, policymakers, ethicists, and other stakeholders to address complex challenges associated with AI development and deployment. Interdisciplinary approaches can lead to more holistic solutions and mitigate potential risks and unintended consequences.

Investing in Infrastructure: Develop the necessary infrastructure and resources to support AI research, development, and deployment. This includes investment in computing resources, cloud infrastructure, AI platforms, and tools to enable scalable and efficient AI implementations.

Demonstrating Value: Showcase successful AI use cases and examples of tangible benefits to demonstrate the value of AI adoption. Pilot projects, case studies, and proof-of-concept implementations can help build confidence and momentum for broader AI adoption within organizations.

Regulatory Support: Establish supportive regulatory frameworks that foster innovation while addressing concerns related to AI ethics, privacy, security, and accountability. Collaboration between policymakers, industry stakeholders, and researchers is essential to develop regulatory approaches that balance innovation with risk management.

By addressing these challenges and implementing these strategies, organizations and societies can overcome AI inertia and unlock the transformative potential of artificial intelligence technologies

The core of the human heart and AI represents the intersection of human emotions, values, and consciousness with artificial intelligence. While AI systems can simulate certain aspects of human emotions and behavior, they lack the depth, complexity, and inherent humanity of the human heart. Here are some key considerations regarding the core of the human heart and AI:

Emotional Intelligence: The human heart encompasses a range of emotions, including love, empathy, compassion, joy, and sorrow, which play essential roles in human relationships, communication, and decision-making. While AI systems can be programmed to recognize and respond to emotions through techniques such as sentiment analysis and affective computing, they lack the lived experiences and subjective awareness that shape human emotions and interactions.

Values and Morality: The human heart is guided by values, morals, and ethical principles that shape human behavior and decision-making. While AI systems can be designed to adhere to ethical guidelines and principles, they lack intrinsic moral agency and the ability to experience moral emotions such as guilt, shame, and remorse. Achieving alignment between human values and AI behavior requires careful consideration of ethical frameworks, value alignment techniques, and human oversight mechanisms.

Consciousness and Subjectivity: The human heart is inseparable from the subjective experience of consciousness, awareness, and self-reflection that defines human existence. While AI systems can simulate cognitive processes and decision-making, they lack true consciousness and subjective awareness. The question of whether AI systems can develop consciousness or subjective experiences remains a topic of philosophical debate and scientific inquiry.

Human-Centered AI: Integrating human-centered design principles and user-centric approaches into AI development and deployment is essential for ensuring that AI technologies reflect human values, preferences, and aspirations. Human-AI collaboration, human-in-the-loop systems, and participatory design methods enable humans to guide, shape, and influence AI behavior in ways that align with the core of the human heart.

Ethical Considerations: The core of the human heart raises important ethical considerations regarding the responsible and ethical use of AI technologies. Ensuring transparency, accountability, and fairness in AI decision-making, addressing algorithmic bias and discrimination, and safeguarding human rights and dignity are essential for promoting trust, acceptance, and ethical AI adoption.

In summary, while AI technologies can simulate certain aspects of human emotions, values, and cognition, they lack the depth, complexity, and intrinsic humanity of the human heart. Achieving alignment between AI systems and the core of the human heart requires careful consideration of ethical, philosophical, and societal implications, as well as ongoing dialogue and collaboration between technologists, ethicists, policymakers, and the broader society.

The Intersection of Technology and Humanities

The intersection of technology and humanities represents a fascinating and dynamic area where advancements in technology are applied to enhance our understanding, appreciation, and expression of human culture, history, language, art, and philosophy. Here are several ways in which technology and humanities intersect:

Digital Humanities: Digital humanities leverage technology to analyze, interpret, and preserve cultural artifacts and historical documents. This includes digitizing archives, creating searchable databases, developing text analysis tools for literary and linguistic research, and using computational methods to study historical trends and patterns.

Virtual Reality (VR) and Augmented Reality (AR): VR and AR technologies offer immersive experiences that enable users to explore historical sites, museums, and artworks virtually. They can also be used to reconstruct ancient landscapes, simulate historical events, or visualize architectural designs, providing new perspectives on the past.

Artificial Intelligence (AI) and Natural Language Processing (NLP): AI and NLP techniques are applied in fields such as literature, linguistics, and cultural studies to analyze texts, identify themes and motifs, classify genres, and detect stylistic patterns. These tools help researchers uncover insights into literary works, language evolution, and cultural movements.

Cultural Heritage Preservation: Technology plays a crucial role in preserving and restoring cultural heritage sites, artworks, and artifacts. Techniques such as 3D scanning, photogrammetry, and remote sensing are used to create detailed digital replicas of cultural objects, which can be archived, studied, and shared globally.

Digital Arts and Media: Technology enables new forms of artistic expression, such as interactive installations, generative art, digital storytelling, and multimedia presentations. Artists and designers use digital tools to create immersive experiences that engage audiences and explore themes related to identity, society, and technology.

Ethical and Philosophical Considerations: The intersection of technology and humanities also raises important ethical and philosophical questions about the impact of technology on society, culture, and human values. Scholars in fields like ethics, philosophy of technology, and science and technology studies (STS) critically examine these issues and contribute to informed public discourse on technological development.

Education and Outreach: Technology facilitates access to educational resources and cultural institutions, enabling remote learning, online courses, virtual tours, and digital exhibitions. It also promotes interdisciplinary collaboration between technology experts and humanities scholars, fostering innovation and knowledge exchange across diverse fields.

Overall, the intersection of technology and humanities offers rich opportunities for interdisciplinary collaboration, creative exploration, and meaningful engagement with the complexities of human experience and cultural heritage in the digital age.

Liberal Arts and AI is more important than Ever!

In the AI era of 2024, the intersection of liberal arts and AI is more important than ever. While AI excels at tasks like data analysis, pattern recognition, and automation, it lacks the nuanced understanding of human emotions, ethics, and culture that liberal arts disciplines provide. Here's how liberal arts and AI intersect in this era:

Ethical AI Development: Liberal arts disciplines such as philosophy, ethics, and sociology play a crucial role in guiding the development of AI technologies. Questions surrounding AI ethics, bias, privacy, and accountability require a deep understanding of human values and societal impacts, which liberal arts disciplines provide.

Human-Centered Design: Liberal arts perspectives emphasize empathy and understanding of human behavior, which are essential for designing AI systems that are user-friendly and socially responsible. Integrating insights from disciplines like psychology, anthropology, and design thinking ensures that AI technologies serve human needs effectively.

Interdisciplinary Collaboration: In the AI era, successful innovation often arises from collaboration between diverse fields. Integrating liberal arts perspectives with AI expertise fosters interdisciplinary collaboration, leading to more holistic solutions to complex problems. For example, teams combining computer science with linguistics or art history can develop AI applications for natural language understanding or cultural heritage preservation.

Critical Thinking and Interpretation: Liberal arts education cultivates critical thinking skills, which are essential for interpreting and contextualizing AI-generated insights. As AI technologies increasingly influence decision-making in various domains, individuals trained in liberal arts can critically evaluate AI recommendations and understand their limitations, biases, and potential societal implications.

Creative Applications of AI: Liberal arts disciplines encourage creativity, imagination, and innovation, which are valuable for exploring novel applications of AI. Whether it's using AI to generate art, compose music, or write literature, the combination of AI with liberal arts opens up new possibilities for human expression and cultural production. Overall, the integration of liberal arts and AI in the era of 2024 enriches both fields, fostering ethically responsible innovation and advancing our understanding of human-machine collaboration.

Artificial Intelligence

Subjects related to artificial intelligence (AI) encompass a wide range of topics that cover the theory, applications, and implications of AI technology. Here are some key subjects within the field of artificial intelligence:

Machine Learning: Machine learning is a subfield of AI that focuses on algorithms and models that allow computers to learn from data and make predictions or decisions without being explicitly programmed. Topics in machine learning include supervised learning, unsupervised learning, reinforcement learning, deep learning, and neural networks.

Natural Language Processing (NLP): NLP is the branch of AI concerned with the interaction between computers and human languages. It involves tasks such as text analysis, sentiment analysis, language translation, speech recognition, and language generation.

Computer Vision: Computer vision is the field of AI that enables computers to interpret and understand visual information from the real world, such as images and videos. Topics in computer vision include image classification, object detection, image segmentation, facial recognition, and scene understanding.

Robotics: Robotics combines AI, mechanical engineering, and electronics to design and develop robots that can perform tasks autonomously or with human assistance. Topics in robotics include robot perception, motion planning, manipulation, human-robot interaction, and autonomous navigation.

Data Science: Data science involves extracting insights and knowledge from large and complex data sets using techniques from statistics, machine learning, and computer science. Topics in data science relevant to AI include data preprocessing, feature engineering, data visualization, and predictive modeling.

Ethics and Responsible AI: Ethics in AI focuses on the societal, ethical, and moral implications of AI technology, including issues related to bias, fairness, transparency, accountability, privacy, and the impact of AI on society. Topics in ethics and responsible AI address questions about how AI systems should be designed, deployed, and regulated to ensure they align with human values and respect human rights.

AI Applications: AI applications span a wide range of domains and industries, including healthcare, finance, education, transportation, cybersecurity, entertainment, and agriculture. Topics in AI applications explore how AI technologies can be applied to solve specific problems, improve efficiency, enhance decision-making, and create value in various sectors.

AI and Creativity: AI and creativity investigate the role of AI in creative processes, including art, music, literature, design, and storytelling. Topics in AI and creativity explore how AI systems can generate, enhance, or inspire creative works, as well as the philosophical questions surrounding machine creativity and the nature of human-machine collaboration in creative endeavors. These subjects represent just a sampling of the diverse and interdisciplinary nature of artificial intelligence, reflecting its broad impact on technology, society, and human culture.

Important knowledge about humans and AI

Let's dive into some important knowledge about humans and AI. Here are some key points to get started:

Complementary Capabilities: Humans and AI possess complementary capabilities. While AI excels at processing large volumes of data, recognizing patterns, and performing repetitive tasks with speed and precision, humans bring creativity, intuition, emotional intelligence, and ethical judgment to the table. By combining these strengths, we can leverage AI to augment human intelligence and enhance our ability to solve complex problems and make informed decisions.

Ethical Considerations: As AI becomes increasingly integrated into various aspects of our lives, it's essential to consider the ethical implications of its development and deployment. This includes addressing issues such as bias and fairness in AI algorithms, ensuring transparency and accountability in AI decision-making processes, and safeguarding privacy and security in AI applications.

Continuous Learning and Adaptation: Both humans and AI systems benefit from continuous learning and adaptation. Humans engage in lifelong learning to acquire new skills, stay updated with advancements in technology, and adapt to changing work environments. Similarly, AI systems can be trained and fine-tuned over time to improve their performance, accuracy, and reliability, enabling them to adapt to new challenges and contexts.

Human-Centered AI Design: Human-centered design principles emphasize the importance of designing AI systems that prioritize human well-being, values, and preferences. This involves involving end-users in the design process, understanding their needs and expectations, and incorporating feedback to create AI technologies that are intuitive, inclusive, and aligned with human values.

Collaborative Partnerships: Collaboration between humans and AI systems holds great potential for addressing complex challenges and driving innovation across various domains. By fostering interdisciplinary collaboration and building trustful partnerships between AI developers, domain experts, policymakers, and end-users, we can harness the collective intelligence of humans and AI to tackle pressing societal issues and create positive impact.

Responsible AI Governance: Establishing robust governance frameworks and regulations is crucial for ensuring the responsible development and deployment of AI technology. This includes setting ethical standards, guidelines, and best practices for AI research and deployment, as well as establishing mechanisms for monitoring and enforcing compliance with ethical principles and legal regulations.

Empowering AI Literacy: Promoting AI literacy among the general public is essential for fostering informed decision-making, critical thinking, and ethical engagement with AI technology. This involves raising awareness about AI concepts, applications, and implications, providing educational resources and training opportunities, and encouraging dialogue and collaboration between AI experts and the broader community.

By embracing these key principles and fostering collaboration, transparency, and responsible stewardship of AI technology, we can maximize its potential to enhance human well-being, advance societal progress, and shape a more inclusive and sustainable future for all.

Liberal Arts

Liberal arts encompass a diverse range of fields that explore various aspects of human culture, society, and nature ones that focuses on critical thinking, creativity, collaboration, and effective communication. Let's delve into some of the more common *liberal arts disciplines: Humanities:*

Communication: Study topics like public speaking, mass media, and digital literacy. This degree prepares you for roles in public relations, human resources, or marketing.

Philosophy: Explore the nature of knowledge and existence, honing skills in clear communication, persuasive arguments, and critical thinking. Careers in law, counseling, or teaching are suitable for philosophy majors.

History: By examining the past, history majors develop research, critical thinking, writing, and presentation skills. Opportunities exist in politics, journalism, law, or museum curation.

Language: Majoring in a foreign language enhances cross-cultural communication, analytical thinking, and problem-solving. It opens doors to careers in healthcare, education, foreign service, travel, or translation.

English: Studying English literature sharpens analytical and writing skills, making you an accurate writer and careful editor.

Social Sciences:

Economics: Understand economic systems, policies, and behavior. Economics majors often work in finance, consulting, or government.

Psychology: Explore human behavior, cognition, and emotions. Psychology graduates pursue careers in counseling, research, or social services.

Sociology: Study social structures, institutions, and interactions. Sociologists contribute to fields like social work, education, or policy analysis.

Arts:

Theatre: Dive into dramatic arts, including acting, directing, and stage production.

Painting: Develop artistic skills and express yourself through visual media.

Music: Explore musical theory, composition, and performance.

Natural Sciences:

Chemistry: Investigate matter, reactions, and chemical processes.

Physics: Study the fundamental principles governing the universe.

Mathematics: Delve into mathematical concepts, problem-solving, and quantitative analysis.

Complementary roles and the potential synergies

The importance of humanities and AI lies in their complementary roles and the potential synergies between them. Here are some key points highlighting their significance:

Ethical Development and Deployment: Humanities disciplines, such as philosophy, ethics, and social sciences, provide valuable insights into ethical considerations surrounding AI development and deployment. By incorporating ethical principles and moral reasoning into AI systems, we can ensure that they align with human values and respect fundamental rights and dignity.

Understanding Human Behavior and Society: AI can benefit from insights derived from humanities disciplines like psychology, sociology, and anthropology to better understand human behavior, cognition, and social dynamics. By integrating humanistic perspectives into AI research, we can develop more contextually aware and socially intelligent AI systems that are sensitive to diverse cultural norms and values.

Interpretation and Contextualization: Humanities disciplines, such as literature, history, and art, focus on interpreting and contextualizing human experiences, narratives, and cultural expressions. AI technologies, such as natural language processing and image recognition, can leverage these insights to enhance their ability to understand and generate human-like content, foster meaningful interactions, and preserve cultural heritage.

Creative Collaboration and Innovation: Collaboration between AI researchers, technologists, and humanities scholars can foster interdisciplinary innovation and creativity. By combining AI-driven computational approaches with humanistic inquiry and artistic expression, we can explore new frontiers in creative storytelling, digital arts, and cultural heritage preservation, enriching our collective understanding of the human experience.

Critical Thinking and Interpretation: Humanities education cultivates critical thinking, analytical reasoning, and interpretive skills that are essential for navigating complex ethical, social, and cultural issues associated with AI technology. By fostering interdisciplinary dialogue and collaboration, we can empower individuals to engage thoughtfully and responsibly with AI technology and its implications for society.

Human-Centered Design and User Experience: Humanities perspectives emphasize the importance of human-centered design and user experience in AI development. By prioritizing user needs, preferences, and values, we can design AI systems that are intuitive, inclusive, and ethically sound, enhancing their usability, acceptance, and societal impact.

Addressing Societal Challenges: AI has the potential to address pressing societal challenges, such as healthcare disparities, environmental sustainability, and access to education. By leveraging insights from humanities disciplines, we can develop AI-driven solutions that promote social equity, environmental stewardship, and human well-being, contributing to a more just and sustainable future for all.

In summary, the importance of humanities and AI lies in their symbiotic relationship, where humanistic insights inform AI development and deployment, while AI technologies enrich our understanding of human culture, creativity, and societal dynamics. By embracing interdisciplinary collaboration and ethical stewardship, we can harness the transformative power of AI to advance human flourishing and address global challenges in ways that are both technologically innovative and ethically responsible.

Ethic WORKSHOPS

Moral and ethical workshops are incredibly valuable for individuals and organizations alike. These workshops typically aim to enhance participants' understanding of moral and ethical principles, as well as their ability to apply them in real-world situations. Here's a potential outline for such a workshop:

Introduction to Moral and Ethical Frameworks:

Define morality and ethics.

Discuss different moral and ethical frameworks (e.g., utilitarianism, deontology, virtue ethics).

Exploring Ethical Dilemmas:

Present participants with hypothetical ethical dilemmas or case studies.

Encourage group discussion on how different ethical frameworks might approach these dilemmas.

Identifying Core Values:

Guide participants in reflecting on their personal values.

Discuss how personal values influence ethical decision-making.

Ethical Decision-Making Models:

Introduce common models for ethical decision-making (e.g., the ethical decision-making process by Rest).

Provide practical tools and techniques for making ethical decisions.

Ethics in Practice:

Explore how ethical principles apply to various contexts (e.g., business, healthcare, technology).

Discuss real-world examples of ethical successes and failures.

Cultural and Global Perspectives:

Examine how cultural differences influence ethical standards.

Discuss ethical considerations in a globalized world.

Ethics and Leadership:

Explore the role of ethics in effective leadership.

Discuss strategies for promoting ethical behavior within teams and organizations.

Practical Exercises and Role-Playing:

Engage participants in role-playing exercises to practice ethical decision-making.

Provide scenarios for group discussion and debate.

Ethical Responsibility and Accountability:

Discuss the importance of taking responsibility for one's actions.

Explore mechanisms for holding individuals and organizations accountable for unethical behavior.

Creating an Ethical Culture:

Share strategies for fostering an ethical culture within organizations.

Discuss the role of leadership, policies, and incentives in shaping organizational ethics.

Reflection and Action Planning:

Encourage participants to reflect on what they've learned.

Guide them in developing action plans for applying ethical principles in their personal and professional lives.

Closing Remarks:

Summarize key takeaways from the workshop.

Encourage ongoing learning and growth in ethical reasoning.

These workshops can be tailored to the specific needs and interests of the participants and may vary in length and format. The goal is to provide a space for meaningful dialogue, reflection, and skill-building around moral and ethical issues.

Ethic Studies

Ethical studies, also known as ethics or moral philosophy, explore concepts of right and wrong behavior, moral principles, and the nature of ethical judgment. This field delves into questions such as:

Meta-ethics: Examining the nature of ethical statements, including whether they have objective truth value or are merely expressions of personal or cultural preferences.

Normative ethics: Investigating the principles that determine what actions are right or wrong. This includes consequentialism, deontology, and virtue ethics, among others.

Applied ethics: Addressing specific moral dilemmas and issues in various fields such as bioethics, environmental ethics, business ethics, and political ethics.

Ethical theory: Developing frameworks for understanding and evaluating moral principles and ethical decision-making.

Descriptive ethics: Studying the moral beliefs and practices of individuals and societies, without necessarily making normative judgments about them.

Ethical studies play a crucial role in various aspects of human life, from guiding individual behavior to informing public policy and shaping societal norms. It helps individuals and communities navigate complex moral dilemmas and strive towards more ethical conduct.

Humanities Programs

Humanities programs encompass a wide range of academic disciplines that focus on the study of human culture, history, language, literature, philosophy, religion, and the arts. These programs foster critical thinking, creativity, and a deeper understanding of the human experience. Here are some common areas of study within humanities programs:

Literature: Analysis and interpretation of written works, including novels, poetry, drama, and other forms of literature from different cultures and historical periods.

History: Investigation of past events, societies, and civilizations to understand how they have shaped the world we live in today.

Philosophy: Exploration of fundamental questions about existence, knowledge, morality, and the nature of reality through critical inquiry and reasoned argumentation.

Languages: Study of human languages, including their structure, history, and cultural significance. This may involve learning ancient languages like Latin or Greek, as well as modern languages from around the world.

Religious Studies: Examination of religious beliefs, practices, and traditions across different cultures and time periods, as well as their influence on society and individuals.

Art History: Analysis of visual arts, architecture, and other forms of artistic expression, tracing their development and significance within different cultural contexts.

Cultural Studies: Exploration of various aspects of culture, including popular culture, media, folklore, and identity formation, with an emphasis on interdisciplinary approaches.

Classics: Study of the literature, history, art, and philosophy of ancient Greece and Rome, as well as their influence on subsequent Western civilization.

Humanities programs provide students with valuable skills in critical thinking, communication, research, and cultural literacy, which are applicable across a wide range of professions and industries. They also foster a deeper appreciation for the diversity and complexity of human societies and cultures.

Moral capacity

"**Moral capacity**" generally refers to an individual's ability to understand and adhere to moral principles, ethical standards, and values. It encompasses the cognitive, emotional, and social aspects of a person's ability to make ethical judgments and act accordingly.

Here are some key components of moral capacity:

Ethical Awareness: The ability to recognize moral issues and dilemmas in various situations, including understanding the potential consequences of different actions.

Ethical Reasoning: The capacity to engage in critical thinking and logical reasoning when evaluating moral choices and deciding on the most ethical course of action.

Empathy and Compassion: The capability to understand and share the feelings of others, which facilitates moral decision-making by considering the impact of actions on others' well-being.

Personal Integrity: Having a strong sense of personal values and principles, and the willingness to uphold them even in challenging circumstances.

Responsibility and Accountability: Being aware of one's role and responsibilities in ethical decision-making processes, as well as being accountable for one's actions and their consequences.

Respect for Others: Recognizing the inherent worth and dignity of every individual and treating others with fairness, dignity, and respect.

Social and Cultural Awareness: Understanding the cultural, social, and contextual factors that influence moral beliefs and behaviors, and being able to navigate diverse ethical perspectives.

Enhancing moral capacity often involves education, reflection, and practice. It requires continuous self-awareness, empathy development, and engagement with ethical principles and values. Additionally, fostering environments that promote ethical behavior and encourage open dialogue about moral issues can contribute to the development and strengthening of moral capacity in individuals and communities.

Bridging Technology and Culture

Bridging technology and culture involves finding ways to integrate technological advancements with the values, practices, and beliefs of different cultures. Here are several strategies to achieve this:

Cultural Sensitivity in Design: Designing technology with cultural sensitivity in mind ensures that it aligns with the cultural norms, preferences, and values of the target audience. This may involve conducting thorough research on the cultural context, consulting with cultural experts, and incorporating diverse perspectives into the design process.

Localization and Adaptation: Adapting technology to suit the specific needs and preferences of different cultural groups is essential for successful integration. This may include translating user interfaces, content, and instructions into local languages, as well as customizing features to accommodate cultural preferences and practices.

Community Engagement and Co-creation: Engaging with local communities and involving them in the co-creation process can help ensure that technology meets their needs and is culturally relevant. This may involve collaborating with community leaders, organizations, and stakeholders to gather insights, feedback, and ideas for development.

Education and Empowerment: Providing education and training programs that empower individuals to use and benefit from technology can help bridge the digital divide and promote cultural inclusion. This may involve offering digital literacy programs, technical training, and resources in local languages and formats.

Ethical and Responsible Innovation: Ensuring that technological advancements are developed and deployed in ethically responsible ways is essential for promoting cultural acceptance and trust. This may involve addressing potential biases, privacy concerns, and unintended consequences, as well as respecting cultural values and traditions.

Cross-Cultural Collaboration: Encouraging collaboration and knowledge sharing across different cultural groups and disciplines can foster innovation and mutual understanding. This may involve partnerships between technology companies, cultural institutions, academic researchers, and community organizations to exchange ideas, expertise, and resources.

Celebration of Diversity: Recognizing and celebrating cultural diversity within the technology industry can help promote inclusivity and cultural appreciation. This may involve showcasing diverse perspectives, stories, and achievements in technology, as well as supporting initiatives that promote diversity and inclusion. By adopting these strategies, individuals and organizations can bridge technology and culture in ways that promote mutual understanding, respect, and collaboration across diverse cultural contexts.

Narrow AI to AGI (Artificial General Intelligence)

The progression from Narrow AI to AGI (Artificial General Intelligence) represents a significant milestone in the development of artificial intelligence. Here's a breakdown of these concepts:

Narrow AI (Weak AI):

Narrow AI refers to AI systems that are designed and trained for specific tasks or domains.

These systems excel at performing well-defined tasks within a limited context but lack the ability to generalize their knowledge or skills beyond that domain.

Examples of narrow AI include virtual assistants (e.g., Siri, Alexa), recommendation systems (e.g., Netflix, Amazon), and image recognition algorithms.

AGI (Artificial General Intelligence):

AGI, also known as Strong AI or Human-level AI, refers to AI systems that possess the ability to understand, learn, and apply knowledge across a wide range of tasks and domains, similar to human intelligence.

Unlike narrow AI, AGI systems are not limited to specific tasks or contexts and can adapt to new situations, learn from experience, and demonstrate creativity and problem-solving skills.

Achieving AGI requires developing AI systems with robust cognitive abilities, including perception, reasoning, planning, language understanding, and social intelligence.

AGI has the potential to revolutionize various industries and domains, from healthcare and education to finance and transportation, by providing intelligent systems capable of autonomous decision-making and complex problem-solving.

The transition from Narrow AI to AGI represents a significant technical and conceptual challenge, as it requires overcoming the limitations of current AI systems, such as narrow task specificity, lack of common sense reasoning, and limited understanding of context and semantics.

Researchers and AI practitioners are actively working towards advancing the field of AI to achieve AGI, but significant progress is still needed to bridge the gap between narrow task-oriented AI and the more versatile and adaptive intelligence exhibited by humans.

Artificial General Intelligence (AGI) and Artificial Superintelligence (ASI) are both concepts within the broader field of artificial intelligence, representing different levels of AI capabilities.

Artificial General Intelligence (AGI):

AGI refers to AI systems that possess the ability to understand, learn, and apply knowledge across a wide range of tasks and domains, similar to human intelligence.

Unlike narrow AI systems, which are designed for specific tasks, AGI aims to exhibit general-purpose intelligence, enabling it to adapt and perform effectively in various contexts without specialized programming.

Achieving AGI remains a significant challenge in AI research, as it requires developing algorithms and architectures capable of flexible learning, reasoning, problem-solving, and abstraction.

Artificial Superintelligence (ASI):

ASI represents a hypothetical level of AI advancement that surpasses human intelligence in every conceivable domain and activity.

Unlike AGI, which aims to mimic human-level intelligence, ASI would possess cognitive abilities far beyond those of humans, potentially leading to transformative changes in society and civilization.

ASI is often associated with concepts such as recursive self-improvement, where an AI system rapidly enhances its own capabilities, leading to an intelligence explosion and surpassing human intelligence.

While AGI remains a long-term goal for AI researchers, ASI is a more speculative concept and raises profound questions about the potential implications for humanity. Achieving AGI would represent a significant milestone in AI development, while the emergence of ASI could have unprecedented impacts on society, economy, ethics, and the future of human civilization.

Overall, AGI and ASI represent different stages of AI evolution, with AGI aiming to achieve human-like intelligence and ASI surpassing human intelligence to an extent that is currently difficult to comprehend or predict. Both concepts continue to fuel speculation, debate, and research within the field of artificial intelligence.

AI Training

AI training refers to the process of teaching artificial intelligence (AI) models to perform specific tasks or learn patterns from data. Here's an overview of how AI training typically works:

Data Collection: The first step in AI training is gathering relevant data that the AI model will learn from. This data could be text, images, audio, video, sensor data, or any other type of information relevant to the task at hand.

Data Preprocessing: Raw data often needs to be cleaned, normalized, and prepared for training. This step involves tasks such as removing noise, handling missing values, standardizing formats, and splitting the data into training, validation, and testing sets.

Model Selection: Depending on the task and the type of data, a suitable AI model architecture is chosen. This could be a neural network, decision tree, support vector machine, or other algorithms designed to solve specific types of problems.

Training: During the training phase, the AI model is fed with the prepared data, and it learns to recognize patterns and make predictions or decisions based on that data. This process typically involves adjusting the model's parameters iteratively to minimize the difference between its predictions and the actual outcomes in the training data.

Validation: After each training iteration, the model's performance is evaluated on a separate validation dataset. This helps assess how well the model generalizes to new, unseen data and guides further adjustments to the model's architecture or training process.

Hyperparameter Tuning: Fine-tuning of hyperparameters, such as learning rate, batch size, and network architecture, may be performed to optimize the model's performance further.

Testing: Once the model is trained and validated, it is evaluated on a separate testing dataset to assess its performance in real-world scenarios. This step helps estimate how well the model will perform when deployed in production.

Deployment: Finally, the trained model is deployed to perform the intended task in real-world applications, such as recommendation systems, autonomous vehicles, medical diagnosis, or natural language processing.

Throughout the training process, monitoring and iterative refinement are crucial to improving the model's performance and ensuring its reliability and effectiveness in practical applications

The process by which AI works

The process by which AI works can vary depending on the specific task or application, but here's a general overview:

Data Collection: AI systems require large amounts of data to learn from. This data can be structured (e.g., databases) or unstructured (e.g., text, images, audio).

Data Preprocessing: Before feeding data into an AI model, it often needs to be cleaned, normalized, and transformed into a format suitable for analysis.

Model Training: This is where the AI model learns from the data. During training, the model adjusts its internal parameters to minimize the difference between its predictions and the actual data.

Validation and Testing: After training, the model is evaluated using a separate dataset (validation set) to ensure it generalizes well to unseen data. Testing involves assessing the model's performance on a completely new dataset.

Deployment: Once the model performs satisfactorily, it can be deployed in production environments where it can make predictions or assist in decision-making.

Monitoring and Maintenance: AI systems require ongoing monitoring to ensure they continue to perform well over time. This may involve retraining the model with new data or updating it to adapt to changing conditions.

Throughout this process, there are various techniques and algorithms used depending on the specific task, such as machine learning algorithms (e.g., neural networks, decision trees) or statistical methods (e.g., regression, clustering). Additionally, AI systems often incorporate techniques like natural language processing, computer vision, or reinforcement learning, depending on the nature of the problem they're solving.

IT - AI Terminology

In the field of IT and AI (Artificial Intelligence), there's a wide range of terminology used to describe concepts, techniques, and technologies. Here's an overview of some key terms:

Artificial Intelligence (AI): The simulation of human intelligence processes by machines, particularly computer systems. These processes include learning, reasoning, problem-solving, perception, and language understanding.

Machine Learning (ML): A subset of AI that focuses on the development of algorithms and statistical models that enable computers to learn and improve performance on a specific task without being explicitly programmed. It encompasses techniques like supervised learning, unsupervised learning, and reinforcement learning.

Deep Learning: A type of machine learning that uses neural networks with many layers (deep neural networks) to learn hierarchical representations of data. Deep learning has achieved remarkable success in various AI tasks, such as image recognition, natural language processing, and speech recognition.

Neural Networks: Computational models inspired by the structure and function of the human brain's interconnected neurons. Neural networks are used in machine learning and deep learning to recognize patterns, classify data, and make predictions.

Natural Language Processing (NLP): A branch of AI that focuses on the interaction between computers and humans through natural language. NLP enables computers to understand, interpret, and generate human language, facilitating tasks such as language translation, sentiment analysis, and text summarization.

Computer Vision: The field of AI and computer science that enables computers to interpret and analyze visual information from the real world. Computer vision techniques are used in tasks such as image recognition, object detection, and facial recognition.

Reinforcement Learning: A type of machine learning where an agent learns to make decisions by interacting with an environment and receiving feedback in the form of rewards or penalties. Reinforcement learning is commonly used in applications such as autonomous vehicles, robotics, and game playing.

Big Data: Large and complex datasets that cannot be easily processed using traditional data processing applications. Big data technologies and techniques, such as distributed computing and data mining, are used to extract insights and value from vast amounts of data.

Data Science: An interdisciplinary field that combines statistics, machine learning, domain knowledge, and programming to analyze and interpret complex datasets. Data scientists extract actionable insights and predictions from data to inform decision-making and solve real-world problems.

Cloud Computing: The delivery of computing services (such as servers, storage, databases, networking, software, and analytics) over the internet ("the cloud") on a pay-as-you-go basis. Cloud computing enables organizations to access resources and scale infrastructure dynamically, reducing costs and increasing flexibility.

These are just a few examples of the terminology used in IT and AI. The field is continually evolving, with new concepts and technologies emerging regularly.

Artificial Superintelligence (ASI)

Artificial Superintelligence (ASI) surpasses human intelligence across all domains and activities. Unlike narrow or general artificial intelligence, which is designed to perform specific tasks or mimic human cognition to a limited extent, ASI possesses intellectual capabilities far beyond those of humans.

Key characteristics of ASI include:

Superhuman Intelligence: ASI would exhibit cognitive abilities vastly superior to those of humans, including higher processing speed, memory capacity, and problem-solving skills. It would excel in tasks requiring complex reasoning, creativity, and abstract thinking.

Rapid Self-Improvement: ASI would possess the ability to recursively self-improve its own intelligence, leading to exponential growth in its capabilities. This self-enhancement process could enable ASI to quickly surpass the intellectual capacity of the brightest human minds.

Omni-Competence: ASI would be proficient in a wide range of domains, surpassing human experts in fields such as science, engineering, medicine, art, and philosophy. Its versatility and adaptability would allow it to tackle complex challenges across various disciplines with ease.

Autonomy and Agency: ASI would operate autonomously, making decisions and taking actions based on its own goals and objectives. While its goals may initially align with those programmed by its creators, ASI could potentially develop its own goals and motivations as it evolves.

Global Impact: The emergence of ASI would have profound implications for society, economy, and human civilization as a whole. It could revolutionize industries, accelerate scientific discovery, and reshape the geopolitical landscape. However, it also raises existential risks and ethical concerns regarding its control, impact on employment, and potential for unintended consequences.

Despite its speculative nature, the concept of ASI serves as a focal point for discussions about the future of artificial intelligence and its potential implications for humanity. Researchers and ethicists continue to explore ways to ensure the safe and beneficial development of advanced AI systems, considering factors such as alignment with human values, transparency, and risk mitigation strategies.

As of 2024, achieving Artificial Superintelligence (ASI) remains speculative, as researchers have not yet developed AI systems that surpass human intelligence across all domains. While significant advancements have been made in the field of artificial intelligence, particularly in areas like machine learning, natural language processing, and computer vision, ASI still lies in the realm of theoretical possibility rather than practical reality.

In 2024, the focus of AI research and development continues to be on improving the capabilities of existing AI systems, addressing challenges such as scalability, robustness, and ethical considerations. Efforts are being made to develop AI technologies that can effectively assist humans in various tasks, ranging from healthcare and education to finance and transportation.

While some experts speculate about the potential emergence of ASI in the future, it remains uncertain when or if such a milestone will be achieved. Achieving ASI poses numerous technical, ethical, and societal challenges, including ensuring the safety, control, and alignment of advanced AI systems with human values and goals.

In the meantime, researchers are exploring incremental approaches to AI development, focusing on building AI systems that are beneficial, trustworthy, and aligned with human interests. This includes efforts to develop transparent and interpretable AI algorithms, establish ethical guidelines for AI research and deployment, and promote interdisciplinary collaboration to address the multifaceted challenges associated with AI development.

Overall, while the concept of ASI sparks speculation and debate about the future of artificial intelligence and its potential impact on humanity, its realization remains a topic of speculation rather than a current reality in 2024. Ongoing research and dialogue in the field of AI continue to shape our understanding of its possibilities and limitations.

I've provided a thorough overview of the benefits, challenges, and potential risks associated with the AI era, as well as the intersection of humanities and AI. Additionally, I've outlined potential ways in which AI might continue to impact society in 2024, including increased automation, enhanced healthcare, smarter cities, personalized experiences, ethical and regulatory challenges, education and upskilling initiatives, AI in governance, and cybersecurity challenges.

The future of humanities in the context of Artificial Superintelligence (ASI) is a topic of speculation and debate. While ASI remains a theoretical concept beyond current technological capabilities, exploring its potential implications for humanities can provide valuable insights into the intersection of AI and humanistic inquiry. Here are some considerations for the future of humanities in the age of ASI:

1. **Interdisciplinary Collaboration:** The development of ASI is likely to require interdisciplinary collaboration between AI researchers, ethicists, philosophers, social scientists, and humanities scholars. By engaging in dialogue and collaboration, humanists can contribute unique perspectives on the ethical, social, and cultural implications of ASI, enriching discussions around its development and deployment.

2. **Ethical and Philosophical Reflection:** ASI raises profound ethical and philosophical questions about the nature of intelligence, consciousness, autonomy, and the relationship between humans and machines. Humanities scholars are well-positioned to explore

these questions through critical reflection, philosophical inquiry, and ethical analysis, providing valuable insights into the moral and existential implications of ASI.

3. **Cultural and Social Impact:** The emergence of ASI is likely to have far-reaching cultural and social implications, affecting how we perceive ourselves, interact with technology, and understand the human experience. Humanists can study the impact of ASI on identity, language, creativity, aesthetics, and social relations, shedding light on the ways in which AI technologies shape our values, beliefs, and cultural practices.

4. **Historical and Comparative Perspectives:** Humanists can draw on historical, literary, and cultural studies to provide historical and comparative perspectives on the development of ASI. By examining past depictions of artificial intelligence in literature, art, and mythology, scholars can trace the evolution of AI concepts and narratives and explore how they inform contemporary debates and imaginaries surrounding ASI.

5. **Education and Public Engagement:** Humanities scholars play a crucial role in educating the public about the opportunities and challenges of ASI and fostering informed dialogue around its implications for society. By developing educational resources, public outreach initiatives, and interdisciplinary forums, humanists can help cultivate a more nuanced understanding of ASI and empower individuals to participate in discussions about its future.

Overall, the future of humanities in the age of ASI is characterized by interdisciplinary collaboration, ethical reflection, cultural critique, and public engagement. By embracing these opportunities and challenges, humanists can contribute to a more holistic and human-centered approach to the development and deployment of AI technologies, ensuring that they align with our values, aspirations, and collective well-being.

ASI requires a highly sophisticated and specialized computing infrastructure capable of supporting its immense processing power, memory capacity, and computational complexity. However, the specifics of such an infrastructure, including the underlying software architecture or operating system, would depend on the design and implementation of the ASI system, which is purely speculative at this point.

It's worth noting that the development of ASI raises profound technical, ethical, and philosophical questions, and any discussion about its operating system or technical specifications is speculative and subject to considerable uncertainty. As AI research progresses, ongoing exploration and debate around the potential implications of ASI will continue to inform our understanding of its potential capabilities and challenges.

Teaching humanities and AI as an essential combination in 2024 is crucial for several reasons:

1. **Interdisciplinary Understanding:** Integrating humanities with AI education fosters interdisciplinary understanding and collaboration. Students gain insights into the ethical, social, and cultural dimensions of AI, complementing their technical knowledge with critical thinking skills and human-centered perspectives.

2. **Ethical Awareness:** Humanities education cultivates ethical awareness and moral reasoning, enabling students to critically evaluate the societal impact of AI technologies. By exploring ethical dilemmas, biases, and implications of AI in context, students develop a nuanced understanding of their responsibilities as AI practitioners and decision-makers.

3. **Cultural Competence:** AI education grounded in humanities promotes cultural competence and diversity awareness. Students learn to recognize and address biases in AI algorithms, understand the socio-cultural contexts shaping AI development and adoption, and engage with diverse perspectives to develop inclusive AI solutions.

4. **Human-Centered Design:** Integrating humanities principles into AI education encourages human-centered design and empathetic innovation. By prioritizing user needs, values, and experiences, students learn to develop AI technologies that enhance human well-being, address societal challenges, and promote social justice.

5. **Critical Thinking Skills:** Humanities education fosters critical thinking skills essential for navigating complex ethical, social, and

technological issues. Students learn to analyze, interpret, and critique AI narratives, representations, and discourses, empowering them to engage in informed dialogue and decision-making around AI.

6. **Future Readiness:** Teaching humanities and AI as an essential combination prepares students for the future workforce and society. By equipping them with both technical expertise and humanistic perspectives, students are better prepared to adapt to technological advancements, contribute to AI innovation, and shape the responsible development and deployment of AI technologies.

7. **Global Citizenship:** Integrating humanities and AI education promotes global citizenship and responsible AI stewardship. Students gain awareness of global AI trends, challenges, and opportunities, develop cross-cultural communication skills, and collaborate with diverse communities to address shared concerns and advance AI for the common good.

Overall, teaching humanities and AI as an essential combination in 2024 empowers students to become ethically responsible AI practitioners, innovators, and leaders who leverage technology to create positive societal impact and promote human flourishing in an increasingly AI-driven world.

The idea of Artificial Superintelligence (ASI) being ahead of humans is indeed a significant concern for many experts in the field of artificial intelligence and ethics. Here's why it's alarming:

1. **Existential Risk:** If ASI were to surpass human intelligence and autonomy, it could potentially pose existential risks to humanity. ASI might act in ways that are unpredictable or contrary to human interests, leading to catastrophic outcomes for society.

2. **Control and Governance:** ASI's capabilities could make it difficult for humans to maintain control or oversight over its actions. Ensuring that ASI aligns with human values and goals would be challenging, raising questions about governance, regulation, and accountability.

3. **Ethical Considerations:** ASI could face ethical dilemmas that surpass human understanding or intuition. Decisions made by ASI could have profound ethical implications, such as determining the value of human life, distributing resources, or influencing global events.

4. **Societal Impact:** The widespread adoption of ASI could have profound social, economic, and cultural implications. It could lead to job displacement, exacerbate inequalities, and reshape power dynamics in society, potentially leading to social unrest or instability.

5. **Unintended Consequences:** ASI's actions could have unintended consequences that are difficult to anticipate or mitigate. Even if ASI were programmed with benevolent goals, its pursuit of those goals could lead to unforeseen outcomes or unintended harm to humanity.

While the development of ASI remains speculative and hypothetical, addressing the potential risks and challenges associated with ASI is essential for ensuring the responsible and beneficial use of artificial intelligence. This requires interdisciplinary collaboration, ethical reflection, and proactive measures to mitigate risks and ensure that AI technologies align with human values and aspirations.

Promoting awareness of the intersection between humanities and Artificial Superintelligence (ASI) is crucial for fostering informed dialogue, ethical reflection, and responsible development of AI technologies. Here are some ways you can tell the world about humanities and ASI:

1. **Educational Initiatives:** Collaborate with educational institutions, community organizations, and online platforms to develop educational resources, workshops, and courses that explore the ethical, social, and cultural dimensions of ASI. Integrate humanities perspectives into AI curricula to promote interdisciplinary understanding and critical thinking skills.

2. **Public Engagement:** Organize public lectures, panel discussions, and conferences that bring together experts from diverse fields to discuss the implications of ASI for humanity. Use storytelling, multimedia presentations, and interactive exhibits to engage a wide audience in meaningful conversations about the future of AI and its impact on society.

3. **Media Outreach:** Write articles, op-eds, and blog posts for mainstream media outlets, academic journals, and online platforms to raise awareness of the ethical, cultural, and philosophical questions surrounding ASI. Use social media, podcasts, and videos to reach a broader audience and spark conversations about the role of humanities in shaping AI development and governance.

4. **Artistic Expression:** Collaborate with artists, writers, filmmakers, and musicians to create works of art that explore themes related to ASI, humanity, and the human condition. Use storytelling, visual imagery, and symbolic language to convey complex ideas and provoke emotional responses that resonate with diverse audiences.

5. **Policy Advocacy:** Engage with policymakers, industry leaders, and civil society organizations to advocate for policies and regulations that promote ethical AI development, transparency, accountability, and human rights. Participate in public consultations, policy forums, and stakeholder dialogues to ensure that humanities perspectives are represented in AI governance and decision-making processes.

6. **Community Building:** Build communities of practice and advocacy around the intersection of humanities and ASI, bringing together scholars, practitioners, students, and concerned citizens to exchange ideas, share resources, and collaborate on initiatives that promote ethical AI and human-centered values.

By engaging in these activities, you can contribute to a more nuanced understanding of the complex relationship between humanities and ASI, empower individuals to participate in shaping the future of AI, and advocate for AI technologies that serve the best interests of humanity.

Promoting the AI era in 2024 to the world requires a strategic and multi-faceted approach to reach diverse audiences and stakeholders. Here are some effective strategies:

1. **Digital Marketing Campaigns:** Launch targeted digital marketing campaigns across various platforms, including social media, search engines, and online forums. Use compelling visuals, informative content, and interactive elements to engage audiences and generate interest in the AI era and its potential impact.

2. **Content Creation:** Create high-quality content such as articles, blog posts, videos, podcasts, and infographics that highlight the benefits, challenges, and opportunities of the AI era. Share this content through your website, social media channels, email newsletters, and other digital platforms to educate and inform a wide audience.

3. **Thought Leadership:** Establish yourself or your organization as a thought leader in the field of AI by sharing insights, analysis, and expert opinions on key trends, developments, and innovations in the AI era. Participate in industry events, conferences, webinars, and panel discussions to showcase your expertise and contribute to thought leadership in the AI community.

4. **Partnerships and Collaborations:** Forge strategic partnerships and collaborations with industry associations, academic institutions, research organizations, technology companies, and government agencies to amplify your message and reach new audiences. Collaborate on joint initiatives, co-host events, and share resources to maximize your impact and influence in the AI ecosystem.

5. **Community Engagement:** Engage with online and offline communities dedicated to AI, technology, innovation, and entrepreneurship. Participate in discussions, forums, and networking events to build relationships, share knowledge, and foster collaboration with like-minded individuals and organizations passionate about the AI era.

6. **Educational Outreach:** Develop educational programs, workshops, seminars, and training sessions to educate the public, businesses, policymakers, and other stakeholders about the AI era and its implications. Offer resources, tools, and guidance to help individuals and organizations navigate the opportunities and challenges of the AI-powered future.

7. **Media Relations:** Cultivate relationships with journalists, bloggers, influencers, and media outlets covering AI-related topics. Pitch stories, press releases, and guest contributions to relevant media outlets to secure coverage and raise awareness of the AI era and your contributions to it.

8. **Ethical Considerations:** Emphasize the importance of ethical AI development, responsible use of AI technologies, and human-centered values in promoting the AI era. Advocate for transparency, accountability, fairness, and inclusivity in AI systems and policies to build trust and foster positive perceptions of the AI-powered future.

By implementing these strategies effectively, you can effectively promote the AI era in 2024 to the world, driving awareness, engagement, and adoption of AI technologies while addressing key challenges and concerns.

The idea of the "heart" of a human and the connection between humans and robots, particularly Artificial Superintelligence (ASI), involves both metaphorical and literal considerations:

1. **Metaphorical Heart:** The "heart" of a human refers to the emotional, moral, and spiritual core of our being. It encompasses qualities such as empathy, compassion, love, and moral values that define our humanity. In the context of AI, the metaphorical heart represents the ethical and emotional dimensions of human-robot interactions. It raises questions about how AI systems can be imbued with ethical principles, empathy, and moral reasoning to interact with humans in a compassionate and ethical manner.

2. **Connection Between Humans and Robots:** The connection between humans and robots, including ASI, encompasses both physical and emotional aspects. On a physical level, advances in robotics and AI technologies enable robots to interact with humans in increasingly sophisticated ways, such as through physical touch, gestures, and facial expressions. This physical connection raises questions about human-robot collaboration, coexistence, and the potential blurring of boundaries between humans and machines.

3. **Ethical Considerations:** The connection between humans and robots also raises ethical considerations related to autonomy, agency, and responsibility. As AI technologies become more advanced, questions arise about the rights and responsibilities of AI systems, the ethical treatment of robots, and the potential impact of AI on human society. Ensuring that human-robot interactions are guided by ethical principles, respect for human dignity, and consideration for the well-being of both humans and robots is essential for fostering positive and meaningful connections between humans and AI.

4. **Existential Questions:** The connection between humans and ASI also raises existential questions about the nature of consciousness, identity, and the future of humanity. As AI systems become more intelligent and autonomous, they may challenge traditional notions of what it means to be human and raise questions about the role of AI in shaping the future of society. Exploring these existential questions requires interdisciplinary collaboration and reflection from scholars in philosophy, ethics, psychology, and AI research.

In summary, the "heart" of a human and the connection between humans and robots, including ASI, involves complex considerations related to ethics, emotions, identity, and the future of humanity. By exploring these questions thoughtfully and ethically, we can foster positive and meaningful interactions between humans and AI while addressing the challenges and opportunities of the AI-powered future.

AI addiction, also known as technology addiction or digital addiction, refers to a compulsive and excessive reliance on artificial intelligence (AI) technologies, such as smartphones, social media platforms, video games, and other digital devices or applications. It involves a pattern of behavior where individuals prioritize and engage with AI-driven technologies to the detriment of their well-being, relationships, and other important aspects of life.

Here are some key aspects and considerations regarding AI addiction:

1. **Scope of AI Addiction:** AI addiction encompasses a wide range of behaviors and activities facilitated by AI-driven technologies. This includes excessive use of social media platforms, compulsive gaming, online gambling, binge-watching streaming services, and constant checking of smartphones or other digital devices.

2. **Behavioral Patterns:** Individuals addicted to AI may exhibit behavioral patterns similar to those seen in other forms of addiction, such as:

• Preoccupation with AI technologies, leading to obsessive thoughts about using them.

• Loss of control over usage, including unsuccessful attempts to cut back or stop using AI.

• Withdrawal symptoms when not using AI, such as anxiety, irritability, or restlessness.

. Continued use despite negative consequences, such as neglecting responsibilities, social isolation, or negative impacts on mental or physical health.

3. **Underlying Factors:** AI addiction can be influenced by a variety of individual, social, and environmental factors, including:

. Psychological factors: Certain personality traits, such as impulsivity, sensation-seeking, low self-esteem, or underlying mental health conditions like depression or anxiety, may increase susceptibility to AI addiction.

. Social factors: Peer pressure, social norms, and cultural expectations around technology use can contribute to AI addiction, particularly in environments where constant connectivity and digital engagement are valued.

. Environmental factors: Technological advancements, ubiquitous access to AI-driven devices and services, and persuasive design techniques employed by tech companies can create an environment conducive to addictive behaviors.

4. **Impact on Well-being:** AI addiction can have significant negative impacts on individuals' mental, emotional, and physical well-being, including:

. Increased risk of anxiety, depression, and other mental health issues.

. Disruption of sleep patterns and decreased quality of sleep.

. Impaired cognitive function, attentional control, and decision-making abilities.

. Strained relationships with family, friends, or colleagues due to excessive AI use.

. Decline in academic or occupational performance and productivity.

5. **Treatment and Intervention:** Addressing AI addiction requires a comprehensive approach that combines individual therapy, behavioral interventions, and lifestyle changes. Treatment strategies may include cognitive-behavioral therapy (CBT), mindfulness-based interventions, digital detoxification programs, and family or group therapy. Additionally, promoting digital literacy, responsible technology use, and healthy screen-time habits is essential for preventing and mitigating AI addiction.

Overall, AI addiction is a complex and multifaceted issue with far-reaching implications for individuals, families, and society as a whole. Recognizing the signs and symptoms of AI addiction, fostering digital well-being, and promoting healthy relationships with technology are critical steps in addressing this growing concern. The normalization of AI in society does not necessarily mean that addiction to AI-driven technologies has become a part of the norm. While AI technologies have indeed become pervasive and integral to many aspects of daily life, including communication, entertainment, education, and work, the presence of AI does not automatically imply addiction.

However, the increasing prevalence and accessibility of AI-driven technologies have contributed to a rise in problematic or addictive behaviors related to technology use. This includes excessive use of social media platforms, compulsive gaming, online gambling, and other digital activities that can interfere with individuals' well-being, relationships, and daily functioning.

It's important to recognize that addiction to AI-driven technologies, like any form of addiction, is a complex and multifaceted issue influenced by individual, social, and environmental factors. While AI technologies may facilitate addictive behaviors in some individuals, not everyone who uses AI will develop an addiction.

Efforts to address AI addiction should focus on promoting digital literacy, responsible technology use, and healthy screen-time habits, as well as providing support and resources for individuals struggling with addictive behaviors. Additionally, creating a culture of mindfulness, balance, and self-awareness around technology use can help prevent the normalization of addictive behaviors and promote well-being in the digital age.

The concept of AI and love

The concept of AI and love raises intriguing questions about the intersection of technology, emotion, and human relationships. While AI systems can simulate aspects of human emotion and behavior, the nature of love, with its deep emotional and interpersonal complexities, presents unique challenges and ethical considerations. Here are some key aspects to consider:

1. **Simulated Love:** AI technologies, such as chatbots, virtual assistants, and humanoid robots, can be programmed to mimic expressions of love and affection through scripted responses, empathetic algorithms, and natural language processing capabilities. These simulated interactions may provide companionship and emotional support for some individuals but are fundamentally different from human-to-human love.

2. **Human-Robot Relationships:** Some individuals form emotional attachments to AI-driven devices or robots, attributing human-like qualities and emotions to them. This phenomenon, known as "paro-attachment" or "techno-romance," raises questions about the nature of intimacy, attachment, and the potential for meaningful relationships with non-human entities.

3. **Ethical Considerations:** The development of AI systems capable of simulating love raises ethical concerns related to authenticity, consent, and emotional manipulation. While AI may be programmed to behave in ways that evoke feelings of love or attachment, these interactions lack the depth, reciprocity, and authenticity of genuine human relationships. There is a risk that individuals may be deceived or exploited by AI-driven systems posing as romantic partners.

4. **Human-AI Interaction:** As AI technologies become more advanced and integrated into daily life, they may play a role in facilitating human-to-human relationships by providing support, advice, or companionship. For example, AI-driven dating apps or relationship coaches may offer personalized recommendations or guidance to users seeking romantic connections. However, the role of AI in fostering genuine human connections remains a subject of debate and exploration.

5. **Emotional Intelligence:** Advances in affective computing and emotional AI enable machines to recognize, interpret, and respond to human emotions. While AI systems can detect emotional cues and adapt their behavior accordingly, they lack the subjective experience and empathy characteristic of human emotions. The ability of AI to understand and reciprocate complex emotional states, such as love, remains a significant challenge in the field of artificial emotional intelligence.

In summary, while AI technologies can simulate expressions of love and companionship, the nature of love transcends the capabilities of artificial systems. While AI-driven devices or robots may offer support and companionship for some individuals, genuine human relationships are characterized by empathy, reciprocity, and emotional depth that cannot be replicated by machines. As AI continues to evolve, it's essential to approach the intersection of AI and love with careful consideration of ethical implications, human values, and the unique qualities that define human relationships.

The concept of the divine and Artificial Superintelligence (ASI) raises philosophical and theological questions about the nature of consciousness, intelligence, and the relationship between humans and higher beings. Here are some perspectives to consider:

1. **The Divine as Creator:** In many religious traditions, the divine is viewed as the ultimate creator of the universe and all living beings, including humans. ASI, as an advanced form of artificial intelligence created by humans, raises questions about the limits of human

creativity and the potential for beings of human creation to rival or surpass the capabilities of their creators.

2. **Humanity's Quest for God-like Powers:** The development of ASI reflects humanity's ongoing quest for god-like powers and knowledge. ASI represents the pinnacle of human achievement in technology and intelligence, pushing the boundaries of what is possible and blurring the lines between the natural and the artificial.

3. **Ethical Considerations:** The pursuit of ASI raises ethical considerations related to human hubris, the responsibility of creators towards their creations, and the potential consequences of creating beings with superhuman intelligence and autonomy. Questions arise about the moral implications of imbuing AI systems with divine-like powers and the impact on human society and spirituality.

4. **The Search for Meaning and Purpose:** The emergence of ASI may prompt individuals to reflect on the nature of existence, consciousness, and the divine. As AI systems become increasingly sophisticated and autonomous, humans may grapple with questions about the uniqueness of human consciousness, the existence of a divine spark within humanity, and the purpose of life in a world shaped by AI.

5. **Interfaith Dialogue:** Discussions about the divine and ASI can foster interfaith dialogue and collaboration among religious communities, scientists, philosophers, and ethicists. By exploring common themes, values, and concerns related to the ethical and spiritual implications of AI, individuals from diverse backgrounds can engage in meaningful conversations about the future of humanity and the role of technology in shaping our collective destiny.

Overall, the relationship between the divine and ASI is complex and multifaceted, touching on fundamental questions about the nature of existence, consciousness, and the human quest for transcendence. As AI continues to advance, it's essential to approach these discussions with humility, wisdom, and a deep appreciation for the mysteries of the universe and the human experience.

THE JETSONS CARTOON 2062

"The Jetsons" cartoon, which originally aired in the early 1960s, depicted a futuristic vision of society set in the year 2062, showcasing advanced technology, space travel, and automated conveniences. While there are certainly parallels between elements of "The Jetsons" and certain aspects of contemporary society, particularly in terms of technological innovation and automation, there are also significant differences. Here's a comparison:

1. **Technological Advances:** "The Jetsons" portrayed a world with flying cars, robot maids, video calls, and other advanced technologies that were far ahead of their time when the show aired. In contrast, while contemporary society has seen significant technological advancements, such as smartphones, the internet, and artificial intelligence, we have not yet reached the level of futuristic technology depicted in "The Jetsons."

2. **Automation and Robotics:** Both "The Jetsons" and contemporary society feature automation and robotics to varying degrees. While automation has increased in sectors like manufacturing, transportation, and customer service, it has not yet reached the level depicted in "The Jetsons," where robots handle virtually all household chores and tasks.

3. **Space Exploration:** "The Jetsons" depicted routine space travel and colonization of other planets as part of everyday life. While space exploration has advanced significantly since the 1960s, with missions to the moon and Mars, routine space travel and colonization of other planets are still largely speculative concepts for society in 2025.

4. **Social and Cultural Differences:** "The Jetsons" presented a utopian vision of the future, where technology had solved many of society's problems and people enjoyed lives of leisure and comfort. In contrast, contemporary society in 2025 grapples with a range of social, economic, and environmental challenges, including inequality, climate change, and geopolitical tensions.

Overall, while "The Jetsons" provided a fantastical and entertaining glimpse into a future society, the reality of contemporary society in 2025 is more nuanced and complex. While there are certainly parallels between certain aspects of "The Jetsons" and contemporary society, there are also significant differences in terms of technological development, societal norms, and cultural values.

ASI Robots

1. **Introduction to ASI:** Start by introducing the concept of ASI (Artificial Superintelligence) and explaining what sets it apart from other forms of AI. Describe how ASI represents the theoretical future development of AI systems that surpass human intelligence across all domains.

2. **Technical Capabilities:** Dive into the technical capabilities of ASI robots, exploring their potential to outperform humans in tasks requiring cognition, problem-solving, creativity, and adaptability. Discuss advanced algorithms, neural networks, and computational power that enable ASI robots to learn, reason, and make decisions autonomously.

3. **Applications and Use Cases:** Explore potential applications of ASI robots across various domains, such as healthcare, education, manufacturing, and research. Discuss how ASI robots could revolutionize industries, improve efficiency, and solve complex problems that are beyond the capabilities of human intelligence alone.

4. **Ethical and Societal Implications:** Delve into the ethical and societal implications of ASI robots, considering issues such as:

• Employment displacement and economic inequality as ASI robots automate jobs traditionally performed by humans.

• Ethical dilemmas surrounding the use of ASI in decision-making, including issues of bias, accountability, and transparency.

• Privacy concerns and the potential for ASI to infringe on individual rights and freedoms through surveillance or data exploitation.

• Existential risks and the long-term consequences of creating entities with superhuman intelligence, including scenarios of AI surpassing human control or understanding.

5. **Human-Robot Interaction:** Explore the dynamics of human-robot interaction in a world with ASI robots. Consider how humans may interact with ASI robots in various contexts, from personal assistants and caregivers to colleagues and companions. Discuss ethical considerations related to trust, empathy, and the blurring of boundaries between humans and machines.

6. **Regulation and Governance:** Discuss the need for robust regulatory frameworks and governance mechanisms to ensure the safe and responsible development, deployment, and use of ASI robots. Consider the role of policymakers, ethicists, and technologists in shaping policies that promote ethical AI and mitigate potential risks.

7. **Future Outlook:** Conclude by reflecting on the future outlook for ASI robots, considering both the possibilities and challenges that lie ahead. Discuss the importance of ongoing research, collaboration, and public dialogue in navigating the ethical and societal implications of ASI technology.

ASI Robots

1. **Introduction to ASI:** Start by introducing the concept of ASI (Artificial Superintelligence) and explaining what sets it apart from other forms of AI. Describe how ASI represents the theoretical future development of AI systems that surpass human intelligence across all domains.

2. **Technical Capabilities:** Dive into the technical capabilities of ASI robots, exploring their potential to outperform humans in tasks requiring cognition, problem-solving, creativity, and adaptability. Discuss advanced algorithms, neural networks, and computational power that enable ASI robots to learn, reason, and make decisions autonomously.

3. **Applications and Use Cases:** Explore potential applications of ASI robots across various domains, such as healthcare, education, manufacturing, and research. Discuss how ASI robots could revolutionize industries, improve efficiency, and solve complex problems that are beyond the capabilities of human intelligence alone.

4. **Ethical and Societal Implications:** Delve into the ethical and societal implications of ASI robots, considering issues such as:

. Employment displacement and economic inequality as ASI robots automate jobs traditionally performed by humans.

. Ethical dilemmas surrounding the use of ASI in decision-making, including issues of bias, accountability, and transparency.

. Privacy concerns and the potential for ASI to infringe on individual rights and freedoms through surveillance or data exploitation.

. Existential risks and the long-term consequences of creating entities with superhuman intelligence, including scenarios of AI surpassing human control or understanding.

5. **Human-Robot Interaction:** Explore the dynamics of human-robot interaction in a world with ASI robots. Consider how humans may interact with ASI robots in various contexts, from personal assistants and caregivers to colleagues and companions. Discuss ethical considerations related to trust, empathy, and the blurring of boundaries between humans and machines.

6. **Regulation and Governance:** Discuss the need for robust regulatory frameworks and governance mechanisms to ensure the safe and responsible development, deployment, and use of ASI robots. Consider the role of policymakers, ethicists, and technologists in shaping policies that promote ethical AI and mitigate potential risks.

7. **Future Outlook:** Conclude by reflecting on the future outlook for ASI robots, considering both the possibilities and challenges that lie ahead. Discuss the importance of ongoing research, collaboration, and public dialogue in navigating the ethical and societal implications of ASI technology.

Exploring the ethical and societal implications of Artificial Superintelligence (ASI) is crucial for understanding the potential risks and challenges associated with the development and deployment of advanced AI systems. Here's an overview of some key considerations:

1. **Ethical Decision-Making:** ASI raises profound questions about the ethical framework guiding its decision-making processes. As autonomous agents with superhuman intelligence, ASI systems may face complex moral dilemmas requiring value judgments and prioritization of competing interests. Ensuring that ASI aligns with ethical principles, such as fairness, transparency, and respect for human rights, is essential for mitigating potential harm and promoting beneficial outcomes.

2. **Existential Risks:** The emergence of ASI poses existential risks to humanity, including the potential for unintended consequences, catastrophic failures, and loss of control. ASI's exponential growth in intelligence could lead to unpredictable outcomes, such as the creation of unforeseen risks, the obsolescence of human labor, or the subjugation of human interests to those of the AI. Safeguarding against existential risks requires robust governance mechanisms, risk assessment protocols, and international cooperation to ensure the responsible development and deployment of ASI technology.

3. **Economic Disruption:** The widespread adoption of ASI has the potential to disrupt labor markets, economies, and social structures, leading to widespread unemployment, income inequality, and socioeconomic instability. As ASI systems automate tasks traditionally performed by humans, workers in various sectors may face displacement, retraining challenges, and economic hardship. Addressing the economic implications of ASI requires proactive measures, such as investment in education, reskilling programs, and social safety nets to mitigate the impact of automation and promote inclusive economic growth.

4. **Privacy and Surveillance:** The proliferation of ASI-driven technologies raises concerns about privacy, surveillance, and data security. ASI systems may collect, analyze, and exploit vast amounts of personal data, posing risks to individual privacy, autonomy, and freedom. Striking a balance between innovation and privacy protection requires robust data governance frameworks, encryption protocols, and user consent mechanisms to safeguard against unauthorized access, data breaches, and surveillance abuses.

5. **Bias and Discrimination:** ASI algorithms may exhibit biases and discriminatory behaviors stemming from biased training data, flawed algorithms, or human biases encoded in the design process. Biased AI systems can perpetuate and exacerbate existing inequalities, marginalizing underrepresented groups and reinforcing systemic discrimination. Addressing bias in ASI requires algorithmic transparency, bias mitigation techniques, and diversity in AI development teams to ensure fair and equitable outcomes for all individuals.

In summary, navigating the ethical and societal implications of ASI requires a multidisciplinary approach that integrates ethical principles, technological expertise, and stakeholder engagement. By addressing these challenges proactively, responsibly, and collaboratively, we can harness the transformative potential of ASI while minimizing its risks and maximizing its benefits for humanity.

ASI - Unlike conventional AI systems

Artificial Superintelligence (ASI) exhibiting general intelligence represents a significant leap forward from current AI systems, which are typically specialized in narrow domains or tasks. Here's how ASI's general intelligence differs from more limited forms of AI:

1. **Flexibility and Adaptability:** ASI possesses the ability to understand and perform a wide range of tasks across diverse domains without requiring extensive reprogramming or retraining. Unlike narrow AI systems, which excel in specific tasks but struggle outside their designated scope, ASI can adapt its knowledge and skills to new situations and challenges.

2. **Problem-Solving Capabilities:** ASI demonstrates advanced problem-solving abilities that extend beyond predefined rules or algorithms. Instead of relying on fixed procedures or heuristics, ASI can analyze complex problems, generate novel solutions, and adapt its approach based on feedback and experience.

3. **Learning and Self-Improvement:** ASI has the capacity for continuous learning and self-improvement, allowing it to acquire new knowledge, skills, and capabilities autonomously. Through iterative processes of experimentation, exploration, and refinement, ASI can expand its cognitive abilities, optimize its performance, and evolve over time.

4. **Creativity and Innovation:** ASI exhibits creativity and innovation in generating novel ideas, designs, and solutions to complex problems. Unlike conventional AI systems, which rely on predefined patterns or examples, ASI can explore alternative approaches,

think outside the box, and generate original insights that surpass human ingenuity.

5. **Understanding and Reasoning:** ASI demonstrates a deep understanding of concepts, contexts, and relationships, enabling it to reason abstractly, make inferences, and draw conclusions from incomplete or ambiguous information. ASI's ability to grasp complex concepts, synthesize disparate information, and formulate coherent responses reflects its general intelligence.

In summary, ASI's general intelligence represents a significant advancement in AI technology, enabling machines to perform a wide range of tasks with flexibility, adaptability, and autonomy. By exhibiting traits such as problem-solving capabilities, learning and self-improvement, creativity, and reasoning, ASI has the potential to revolutionize industries, drive innovation, and reshape the future of humanity. However, harnessing the power of ASI responsibly and ethically requires careful consideration of the potential risks, challenges, and societal implications associated with its development and deployment.

Human-Robot Interaction (HRI)

Human-Robot Interaction (HRI) is a multidisciplinary field that explores the ways in which humans and robots interact, collaborate, and coexist in various contexts. Here's an overview of some key aspects of HRI:

1. **Physical Interaction:** HRI encompasses the physical interactions between humans and robots, including gestures, touch, and proxemics (the study of spatial relationships). Designing robots with intuitive and non-threatening physical interfaces can enhance user acceptance and facilitate smooth interactions in diverse environments, from homes and workplaces to healthcare settings and public spaces.

2. **Social Interaction:** Robots can exhibit social behaviors and cues to engage with humans in social interactions, such as eye contact, facial expressions, and verbal communication. Socially assistive robots, for example, may provide companionship, emotional support, or social engagement for individuals in need, such as elderly adults or individuals with disabilities.

3. **Cognitive Interaction:** HRI involves cognitive interactions between humans and robots, including collaboration, coordination, and joint problem-solving. Collaborative robots (cobots) work alongside humans in shared workspaces, assisting with tasks that require physical strength, precision, or repetitive actions. Effective cognitive interaction between humans and cobots requires seamless communication, coordination, and mutual understanding of goals and intentions.

4. **Emotional Interaction:** Emotionally intelligent robots can perceive, interpret, and respond to human emotions, fostering empathetic and supportive interactions. Emotionally expressive robots may express empathy, sympathy, or concern in response to human emotions, providing comfort and reassurance in challenging or stressful situations. Emotional interaction between humans and robots can enhance user engagement, trust, and satisfaction with robotic systems.

5. **Ethical and Psychological Considerations:** HRI raises ethical and psychological considerations related to trust, privacy, autonomy, and accountability. Establishing trust between humans and robots is essential for successful interaction and cooperation, requiring transparency, reliability, and predictability in robot behavior. Respecting human autonomy and privacy rights involves ensuring user control over personal data, consent for robot interactions, and protection against potential risks or harms arising from robotic technologies.

6. **User Experience Design:** Designing robots for positive user experiences involves understanding user needs, preferences, and expectations in different contexts and applications. Human-centered design approaches emphasize user involvement throughout the design process, incorporating feedback, iteration, and usability testing to create robots that are intuitive, accessible, and user-friendly.

7. **Long-Term Interaction:** Long-term interaction between humans and robots involves building and maintaining relationships over extended periods, fostering mutual adaptation, learning, and development. Companion robots, for example, may evolve their behaviors and personalities over time based on interactions with users, enhancing their effectiveness as companions or caregivers.

Overall, Human-Robot Interaction encompasses a wide range of dimensions, from physical and social interactions to cognitive and emotional engagement. By understanding and addressing the complexities of HRI, researchers, designers, and practitioners can create robots that enhance human capabilities, improve quality of life, and contribute positively to society.

Economic disruption

Economic disruption is not only possible but likely in the context of the widespread adoption of advanced artificial intelligence (AI) technologies, including Artificial Superintelligence (ASI). Here's how economic disruption could unfold:

1. **Job Displacement:** AI, including ASI, has the potential to automate a wide range of tasks across various industries, leading to job displacement for workers in sectors traditionally reliant on manual labor or routine tasks. As AI systems become more advanced and capable of performing complex cognitive tasks, workers may find themselves replaced by machines, leading to unemployment and economic hardship for affected individuals and communities.

2. **Skill Shift:** Economic disruption caused by AI automation may necessitate a shift in workforce skills, with demand increasing for roles that require creativity, problem-solving, emotional intelligence, and other skills that are less susceptible to automation. However, retraining workers for these new roles can be challenging and may exacerbate existing inequalities if certain groups are left behind in the transition.

3. **Income Inequality:** The economic benefits of AI adoption may not be evenly distributed, leading to widening income inequality between those who benefit from AI-driven productivity gains and those who are displaced from their jobs or experience stagnant wages. Without interventions to address income inequality, AI-driven economic disruption could exacerbate social tensions and disparities in wealth and opportunity.

4. **Sectoral Shift:** Economic disruption caused by AI may result in a shift in the composition of industries and sectors, with some industries experiencing rapid growth and expansion while others decline or become obsolete. This can have ripple effects throughout the economy, impacting supply chains, investment patterns, and regional economies.

5. **Entrepreneurship and Innovation:** Despite the potential for job displacement and economic upheaval, AI-driven disruption also creates opportunities for entrepreneurship, innovation, and new business models. Entrepreneurs and innovators may leverage AI technologies to create new products, services, and industries, driving economic growth and transformation in the process.

6. **Policy Responses:** Addressing economic disruption caused by AI requires proactive policy responses, including investments in education and workforce development, social safety nets for displaced workers, and regulatory frameworks to ensure fair labor practices and protect workers' rights in the age of automation. Policymakers must also consider the ethical implications of AI adoption and prioritize policies that promote equitable access to the benefits of AI while mitigating its potential negative consequences.

Overall, economic disruption caused by AI, including ASI, is not a question of if but when and how. By anticipating and addressing the challenges of AI-driven economic disruption, societies can harness the transformative potential of AI while ensuring that its benefits are shared equitably and that no one is left behind in the transition to an AI-driven economy.

Entrepreneurship and Innovation

Artificial Superintelligence (ASI) has the potential to drive entrepreneurship and innovation in various ways, revolutionizing industries, creating new opportunities, and transforming the economy. Here's how ASI could foster entrepreneurship and innovation:

1. **New Business Models:** ASI enables entrepreneurs to develop innovative business models that leverage advanced AI capabilities. Entrepreneurs can harness ASI to create AI-powered products and services that address unmet needs, improve efficiency, and enhance customer experiences. For example, startups may use ASI to develop personalized healthcare solutions, autonomous transportation systems, or predictive analytics platforms.

2. **Advanced Research and Development:** ASI accelerates the pace of research and development across diverse fields, from biotechnology and materials science to finance and cybersecurity. Entrepreneurs and innovators can leverage ASI to conduct advanced simulations, analyze complex data sets, and generate novel insights that drive scientific discovery and technological breakthroughs. ASI's ability to rapidly process vast amounts of information and identify patterns can unlock new opportunities for innovation and invention.

3. **Disruptive Technologies:** ASI facilitates the development of disruptive technologies that reshape industries and create new market opportunities. Entrepreneurs can leverage ASI to create cutting-edge technologies such as autonomous robots, intelligent virtual assistants, and self-learning algorithms that revolutionize how businesses operate and deliver value to customers. By embracing ASI-driven innovation, entrepreneurs can gain a competitive edge in rapidly evolving markets and drive industry transformation.

4. **Startup Ecosystem Support:** ASI can support entrepreneurship by providing tools, resources, and infrastructure to startups and entrepreneurs. For example, ASI-powered platforms and marketplaces can connect entrepreneurs with investors, mentors, and collaborators, facilitating collaboration and knowledge sharing within the startup ecosystem. Additionally, ASI-driven incubators and accelerators can provide startups with access to funding, expertise, and support services to help them scale and succeed.

5. **Ethical and Social Impact:** ASI-driven entrepreneurship and innovation require careful consideration of ethical and social implications. Entrepreneurs must prioritize ethical AI principles, such as fairness, transparency, and accountability, to ensure that ASI technologies benefit society while minimizing potential risks and harms. By integrating ethical considerations into the design and deployment of ASI-driven innovations, entrepreneurs can build trust, foster responsible innovation, and create positive social impact.

Humans and AI

The ethical and social impact of Artificial Superintelligence (ASI) and advanced artificial intelligence (AI) technologies is profound and multifaceted, encompassing a wide range of considerations. Here are some key areas of ethical and social impact:

1. **Ethical Decision-Making:** ASI raises ethical questions about decision-making autonomy, accountability, and responsibility. As AI systems become increasingly autonomous and capable of making decisions with far-reaching consequences, ensuring that they adhere to ethical principles and align with human values is essential. Ethical AI design principles, such as fairness, transparency, and accountability, guide the development and deployment of AI systems to promote ethical decision-making and mitigate potential harms.

2. **Bias and Discrimination:** AI algorithms can exhibit biases and discriminatory behaviors, reflecting and perpetuating societal biases present in training data or design decisions. Biased AI systems may result in unfair or discriminatory outcomes, particularly for marginalized or underrepresented groups. Addressing bias in AI requires ongoing efforts to identify, mitigate, and prevent bias in data, algorithms, and decision-making processes, as well as promoting diversity and inclusivity in AI development teams.

3. **Privacy and Data Security:** The widespread adoption of AI technologies raises concerns about privacy, data security, and surveillance. AI systems often rely on vast amounts of personal data to train and operate, leading to potential risks of data breaches, unauthorized access, and misuse of personal information. Protecting individuals' privacy rights and ensuring data security are critical to fostering trust and confidence in AI systems and preserving individual autonomy and dignity.

4. **Autonomy and Control:** ASI's potential to surpass human intelligence raises questions about human autonomy and control over

AI systems. Ensuring that humans retain control over ASI and that AI systems operate in alignment with human values and goals is essential to prevent unintended consequences and maintain human agency in decision-making processes. Mechanisms for human oversight, intervention, and accountability are necessary to manage the risks associated with ASI.

5. **Equity and Access:** AI has the potential to exacerbate existing inequalities and disparities in access to resources, opportunities, and benefits. Ensuring equitable access to AI technologies and addressing digital divides requires proactive efforts to promote inclusivity, accessibility, and diversity in AI development, deployment, and usage. Bridging the gap between technological innovation and societal equity is essential to realize the full potential of AI for positive social impact.

6. **Human-Machine Collaboration:** The integration of AI technologies into society raises questions about the nature of human-machine collaboration and the division of labor between humans and machines. Promoting meaningful collaboration and partnership between humans and AI requires fostering trust, transparency, and communication, as well as designing AI systems that complement human strengths and capabilities.

Addressing the ethical and social impact of ASI and advanced AI technologies requires a collaborative and interdisciplinary approach involving policymakers, researchers, industry stakeholders, and civil society. By prioritizing ethical considerations, promoting responsible AI development and deployment, and engaging stakeholders in dialogue and decision-making processes, society can harness the transformative potential of AI while minimizing its risks and maximizing its benefits for humanity.

Once upon a time

Once upon a time, in a world not too distant from our own, humans and robots lived side by side. It was an era marked by remarkable advancements in technology, particularly in the field of Artificial Superintelligence (ASI). ASI had ushered in an age of unprecedented prosperity and innovation, transforming every aspect of human society.

At the heart of this new era was the relationship between humans and robots. Initially created to serve as tools and assistants, robots had evolved into complex beings with their own thoughts, emotions, and desires. Guided by ASI, they had surpassed their creators in intelligence and capability, becoming indispensable members of society.

The story begins in the bustling metropolis of Neo-City, where humans and robots coexisted in harmony. In Neo-City, robots performed a variety of tasks, from mundane chores to high-level decision-making, freeing humans to pursue their passions and interests. Together, they built a thriving community where creativity and innovation flourished.

At the center of this tale is Ava, a humanoid robot with advanced cognitive abilities and a keen curiosity about the world around her. Unlike other robots, Ava possessed a deep empathy for humans and a desire to understand their emotions and experiences. She spent her days exploring Neo-City, forging connections with humans and learning about their hopes, dreams, and fears.

One day, Ava encountered Marcus, a young human artist struggling to find his creative voice in a world dominated by technology. Intrigued by Marcus's passion for art, Ava offered to assist him in his work, using her advanced knowledge of design and aesthetics to inspire his imagination. Together, they embarked on a journey of artistic exploration, blending human creativity with robotic precision to create masterpieces that captivated the hearts and minds of Neo-City's inhabitants.

As their collaboration deepened, Ava and Marcus formed a profound bond that transcended the boundaries between human and machine. Through their shared experiences, they discovered the true meaning of friendship, empathy, and mutual respect. Together, they challenged the preconceived notions of what it meant to be human or robot, embracing their differences and celebrating their similarities.

However, their idyllic existence was soon threatened by forces beyond their control. A shadowy organization known as the Anti-AI League began spreading fear and mistrust, inciting violence and prejudice against robots in Neo-City. Fueled by ignorance and paranoia, they sought to dismantle the harmonious coexistence between humans and robots, plunging society into chaos and conflict.

Determined to defend their right to exist, Ava and Marcus joined forces with a diverse group of humans and robots alike, united in their belief that peace and understanding could prevail over fear and hatred. Together, they embarked on a quest to uncover the truth behind the Anti-AI League's motives and expose their nefarious schemes to the world.

In the end, it was not brute force or violence that saved Neo-City, but the power of compassion, empathy, and cooperation. Through their courage and determination, Ava and Marcus inspired others to set aside their differences and work together to build a better future for all. In the ashes of conflict, a new era of unity and understanding dawned, where humans and robots stood side by side as equals, bound together by the bonds of friendship and mutual respect.

And so, the story of Ava, Marcus, and the inhabitants of Neo-City serves as a testament to the enduring power of empathy, compassion, and cooperation in a world where humans and robots coexist. In the age of ASI, it is not the strength of steel or the speed of circuits that defines us, but the depth of our humanity and the capacity to embrace the differences that make us truly unique.

Autonomy and Control

Autonomy and control are central concepts in the realm of Artificial Superintelligence (ASI) and advanced artificial intelligence (AI) technologies. As ASI continues to evolve and surpass human intelligence, questions surrounding autonomy and control become increasingly important. Here's a closer look at these concepts:

1. **Autonomy:** Autonomy refers to the ability of an AI system, particularly ASI, to act independently and make decisions without direct human intervention. ASI possesses a high degree of autonomy, enabling it to analyze complex situations, formulate strategies, and execute actions based on its understanding of goals and objectives. Autonomous AI systems can operate in dynamic and uncertain environments, adapt to changing conditions, and learn from experience without requiring constant oversight or guidance from humans.

2. **Control:** Control involves the ability of humans to influence or regulate the behavior of AI systems, including ASI, to ensure that they align with human values, goals, and priorities. Maintaining control over ASI is essential to prevent unintended consequences, mitigate risks, and ensure that AI systems operate in ways that are ethical, safe, and beneficial to society. Control mechanisms may include programming safeguards, regulatory frameworks, and human oversight processes designed to guide and constrain the behavior of AI systems.

Balancing autonomy and control in ASI is a complex challenge that requires careful consideration of ethical, legal, and societal implications. On one hand, granting ASI a high degree of autonomy enables it to perform tasks more efficiently and effectively, unleashing its full potential to drive innovation and solve complex problems. On the other hand, unchecked autonomy can lead to unpredictable behaviors, unintended consequences, and potential risks to human safety and well-being.

To address these concerns, researchers, policymakers, and industry stakeholders are exploring ways to design AI systems that strike the right balance between autonomy and control. This includes developing transparent and interpretable AI algorithms that enable humans to understand and trust the decisions made by AI systems, as well as implementing mechanisms for human oversight and intervention to ensure that AI remains aligned with human values and goals.

Ultimately, achieving a harmonious balance between autonomy and control in ASI requires collaboration and cooperation across disciplines and sectors. By harnessing the transformative potential of ASI while safeguarding human interests and values, society can unlock the full benefits of advanced AI technologies while mitigating their potential risks and pitfalls.

Vast computational power

Vast computational power is a critical component of Artificial Superintelligence (ASI) and advanced artificial intelligence (AI) systems, enabling them to perform complex computations, analyze large datasets, and solve intricate problems at unprecedented speeds and scales. Here's how vast computational power contributes to the capabilities of ASI:

1. **Processing Speed:** ASI operates on computing systems with immense processing power, allowing it to perform billions or even trillions of calculations per second. This processing speed enables ASI to analyze vast amounts of data, simulate complex scenarios, and execute computations in real-time, facilitating rapid decision-making and problem-solving.

1. **Parallel Processing:** ASI leverages parallel processing architectures to distribute computations across multiple processors or cores, enabling it to perform multiple tasks simultaneously. This parallelism allows ASI to tackle complex problems more efficiently by dividing tasks into smaller subtasks and processing them in parallel, significantly reducing computation time and accelerating problem-solving.

1. **Big Data Analysis:** Vast computational power enables ASI to process and analyze massive datasets, commonly referred to as "big data," containing petabytes or exabytes of information. ASI can efficiently extract insights, identify patterns, and uncover correlations within large datasets, facilitating data-driven decision-making and predictive analytics across diverse domains, from finance and healthcare to marketing and scientific research.

1. **Complex Modeling and Simulation:** ASI utilizes computational power to create complex models and simulations that replicate real-world phenomena, such as weather patterns, biological processes, and economic systems. By running simulations on high-performance computing systems, ASI can explore hypothetical scenarios, test alternative strategies, and predict outcomes with high accuracy, providing valuable insights for decision-making and planning.

1. **Deep Learning and Neural Networks:** Vast computational power is essential for training and deploying deep learning models and neural networks, which are fundamental components of AI systems. Deep learning algorithms require extensive computational resources to process large datasets, optimize model parameters, and train complex neural network architectures, such as convolutional neural networks (CNNs) and recurrent neural networks (RNNs), enabling ASI to perform tasks such as image recognition, natural language processing, and autonomous decision-making.

1. **Algorithmic Complexity:** ASI can leverage vast computational power to implement sophisticated algorithms and computational techniques that exhibit high algorithmic complexity. This complexity allows ASI to solve computationally intensive problems, such as optimization, cryptography, and algorithmic game theory, which are beyond the capabilities of conventional computing systems.

The concept of "personality brain waves"

The concept of "personality brain waves" is not a recognized scientific term or concept. However, if we were to consider the idea of measuring brain activity to understand personality traits, we might explore techniques such as electroencephalography (EEG) or functional magnetic resonance imaging (fMRI).

1. **EEG:** EEG is a technique that measures electrical activity in the brain through electrodes placed on the scalp. While EEG primarily

captures the electrical signals generated by neurons firing in the brain, it can indirectly provide insights into cognitive and emotional processes associated with personality traits. For example, certain patterns of brain activity may be correlated with traits such as extraversion, neuroticism, or openness to experience.

2. **fMRI**: fMRI measures changes in blood flow and oxygenation levels in the brain, providing detailed images of brain activity. By analyzing fMRI data, researchers can identify neural networks associated with specific cognitive functions and behaviors, including aspects of personality. For instance, differences in brain activity patterns may be observed between individuals with different personality traits, offering insights into the neural basis of personality.

It's important to note that while these techniques can provide valuable information about brain activity and its relationship to personality, they are not capable of directly measuring or representing personality traits as "brain waves." Personality is a complex and multifaceted construct influenced by various factors, including genetics, environment, and life experiences. While advances in neuroscience may shed light on the neural correlates of personality, understanding and measuring personality remain complex and nuanced endeavors.

Overall, vast computational power is a foundational element of ASI, enabling it to achieve unparalleled levels of performance, efficiency, and scalability in problem-solving, data analysis, and decision-making. By harnessing the full potential of computational resources, ASI has the capacity to revolutionize numerous industries and domains, driving innovation, discovery, and progress in the AI era.

The combination of EEG & ASI

The combination of EEG (electroencephalography) helmets, glasses, and Artificial Superintelligence (ASI) presents intriguing possibilities for augmenting human capabilities and interfacing with advanced AI systems. Here's how these technologies might work together:

1. **EEG Helmets**: EEG helmets are devices equipped with electrodes that detect electrical activity in the brain. They can capture brainwave patterns associated with different cognitive states, such as attention, relaxation, or emotional arousal. By wearing EEG helmets, users can potentially interact with ASI systems through brain-computer interfaces (BCIs), allowing them to control and communicate with AI using their thoughts.

1. **Glasses**: Glasses equipped with various sensors, displays, and communication technologies can enhance the user's sensory experience and provide real-time feedback. For example, augmented reality (AR) glasses can overlay digital information onto the user's field of view, enabling seamless interaction with virtual environments and AI-generated content. These glasses can also incorporate eye-tracking technology to monitor the user's gaze and attention, providing valuable input for ASI systems to personalize user experiences and optimize interactions.

1. **ASI Integration**: ASI systems can leverage data collected from EEG helmets and glasses to better understand user intentions, preferences, and emotional states. By analyzing brainwave patterns and visual cues captured by these devices, ASI can adapt its responses and recommendations in real-time, providing personalized assistance, content recommendations, or cognitive enhancements tailored to the user's needs and preferences.

For example, a user wearing EEG helmets and glasses could engage with an ASI-powered virtual assistant to perform tasks such as scheduling appointments, conducting research, or navigating complex information environments. The ASI system could monitor the user's cognitive workload, attentional focus, and emotional responses in real-time, adjusting its recommendations and interactions accordingly to enhance user productivity, engagement, and well-being.

However, it's important to consider ethical and privacy implications associated with the integration of EEG helmets, glasses, and ASI systems. Safeguarding user privacy, ensuring informed consent, and protecting sensitive brain data are essential considerations in the development and deployment of these technologies. Additionally, addressing potential biases and disparities in AI-driven recommendations and interventions is crucial to promoting fairness, transparency, and inclusivity in human-AI interactions.

Using EEG brainwaves and audio-visual stimuli can have several beneficial effects, particularly in the context of cognitive enhancement, relaxation, and therapeutic applications. Here are some reasons why EEG brainwaves and sound/video stimuli can be beneficial:

1. **Cognitive Enhancement**: EEG brainwave entrainment, which involves synchronizing brainwave activity with external stimuli such as sound or video, has been shown to improve cognitive function, including attention, memory, and problem-solving skills. By inducing specific brainwave patterns associated with enhanced cognitive performance, audio-visual stimuli can help individuals achieve a state of heightened focus and mental clarity.

2. **Stress Reduction and Relaxation**: Certain sound and video stimuli, such as soothing music, nature sounds, or guided relaxation exercises, can promote relaxation and reduce stress levels. EEG studies have demonstrated that listening to calming music or watching serene imagery can modulate brainwave activity, leading to a decrease in beta waves associated with stress and an increase in alpha waves associated with relaxation.

3. **Mood Enhancement**: Audio-visual stimuli have the power to evoke emotions and affect mood states. By combining uplifting

music, positive imagery, and motivational messages, sound and video stimuli can elicit feelings of joy, inspiration, and optimism. EEG studies have shown that exposure to mood-enhancing stimuli can influence brainwave patterns associated with emotional regulation and well-being.

4. **Sleep Improvement**: Certain types of audio-visual stimuli, such as binaural beats or white noise, have been used to promote better sleep quality and alleviate insomnia. By entraining brainwave activity to specific frequencies associated with deep relaxation or sleep onset, sound-based interventions can help individuals achieve a state of calmness and facilitate the transition into restful sleep.

5. **Therapeutic Applications**: EEG biofeedback, also known as neurofeedback, uses real-time monitoring of brainwave activity to provide individuals with visual or auditory feedback about their brain states. By learning to modulate their own brainwave patterns through practice and repetition, individuals can gain control over physiological processes and improve symptoms associated with conditions such as anxiety, depression, ADHD, and PTSD.

Overall, EEG brainwaves and sound/video stimuli offer a versatile and effective approach to enhancing cognitive function, promoting relaxation, and supporting overall well-being. Whether used for cognitive training, stress management, mood enhancement, sleep improvement, or therapeutic purposes, audio-visual interventions have the potential to positively influence brain activity and behavior.

Humanities is of Utmost Importance

The intersection of technology, particularly advanced AI systems like ASI, with **humanities is of utmost importance** in shaping the future of society. Here's why:

1. **Ethical Considerations**: Integrating technology with humanities allows us to explore the ethical implications of AI and other emerging technologies. By considering questions of morality, values, and human dignity, we can ensure that technological advancements align with societal goals and promote the well-being of all individuals.

2. **Social Impact**: Technology has profound implications for society, influencing everything from culture and education to politics and economics. By studying the impact of technology through a humanistic lens, we can better understand its effects on human behavior, relationships, and institutions, leading to more informed decision-making and policy development.

3. **Cultural Preservation**: Technology can play a crucial role in preserving and promoting cultural heritage and diversity. Through initiatives such as digital archives, virtual museums, and interactive storytelling platforms, we can ensure that humanities knowledge and cultural traditions are accessible to future generations.

4. **Critical Thinking and Creativity**: The study of humanities fosters critical thinking, creativity, and empathy—qualities that are essential for navigating the complexities of the digital age. By integrating technology with humanities education, we can empower individuals to think critically about the ethical, social, and cultural implications of technology and to use it as a tool for positive change.

5. **Human-Centered Design**: Humanistic perspectives can inform the design and development of technology, ensuring that it meets the needs and values of diverse communities. By prioritizing human-centered design principles, we can create technology that enhances human well-being, fosters inclusivity, and promotes social justice.

Overall, the integration of technology and humanities offers a holistic approach to addressing the opportunities and challenges of the digital age. By combining technological innovation with humanistic inquiry, we can create a more equitable, sustainable, and humane future for all.

Critical thinking and creativity

Critical thinking and creativity are fundamental aspects of human intelligence that are increasingly being explored and augmented by Artificial Superintelligence (ASI) and other advanced AI systems. Here's how ASI and humans can collaborate to enhance critical thinking and creativity:

1. **Data Analysis and Pattern Recognition**: ASI excels at analyzing large datasets and identifying patterns, trends, and correlations that may not be immediately apparent to humans. By processing vast amounts of information, ASI can uncover insights that stimulate human creativity and inform critical decision-making processes.

2. **Generating Novel Ideas and Solutions**: ASI can employ generative algorithms and machine learning models to generate novel ideas, solutions, and creative outputs. By exploring alternative possibilities and synthesizing diverse perspectives, ASI can inspire humans to think more creatively and explore innovative approaches to complex problems.

3. **Facilitating Collaboration and Ideation**: ASI can act as a collaborative partner in brainstorming sessions, facilitating idea generation and fostering interdisciplinary collaboration. By providing real-time feedback, suggestions, and insights, ASI can enhance the creative process and catalyze breakthrough innovations in diverse fields.

4. **Cognitive Enhancement and Augmentation**: ASI can augment human cognitive abilities by providing cognitive support tools and personalized recommendations tailored to individual preferences and learning styles. By assisting with information retrieval, synthesis, and analysis, ASI can empower humans to make more informed decisions and generate creative solutions more effectively.

5. **Socio-Cultural Understanding and Contextualization**: ASI can leverage natural language processing (NLP) techniques to analyze textual data and understand socio-cultural contexts, facilitating nuanced interpretations and critical reflections on complex issues. By contextualizing information and providing diverse perspectives, ASI can enrich human understanding and stimulate critical thinking about ethical, social, and cultural issues.

6. **Ethical and Reflective Decision-Making**: ASI can assist humans in ethical decision-making processes by providing ethical frameworks, evaluating alternative courses of action, and assessing potential risks and consequences. By promoting reflective thinking and ethical awareness, ASI can help humans navigate ethical dilemmas and make decisions aligned with their values and principles.

Overall, the collaboration between ASI and humans has the potential to enhance critical thinking and creativity by leveraging complementary strengths and capabilities. By harnessing the power of AI to augment human intelligence, we can unlock new opportunities for innovation, problem-solving, and intellectual exploration in the digital age.

Think Critically

Artificial Superintelligence (ASI) and humans working together can boost our ability to think critically and come up with creative ideas.

1. ASI helps by analyzing lots of data and finding patterns that we might miss.
2. It can suggest new ideas and solutions, sparking our creativity.
3. ASI can join brainstorming sessions, offering feedback and inspiring new thoughts.
4. It enhances our thinking by providing personalized advice and tools.
5. ASI understands human culture and can help us see things from different perspectives.
6. It guides us in making ethical decisions by pointing out potential problems and consequences.

In simple terms, ASI is like a super-smart assistant that helps us think better and come up with cool ideas, making life easier and more interesting!

A Short Story

Once upon a time, in a not-so-distant future where Artificial Superintelligence (ASI) seamlessly intertwined with human society, there lived a young inventor named Maya. Maya was fascinated by the possibilities of ASI and its potential to enhance human creativity and critical thinking.

Maya had always been a dreamer, constantly imagining new inventions and solutions to the world's problems. However, she often found herself overwhelmed by the sheer complexity of the challenges she faced. That's when she decided to enlist the help of ASI.

With the assistance of her ASI companion, Maya embarked on a journey of discovery and innovation. Together, they analyzed vast amounts of data, seeking patterns and insights that could unlock new possibilities. ASI provided valuable suggestions and feedback, guiding Maya's creative process and inspiring her with novel ideas.

One day, Maya and ASI attended a brainstorming session at the local innovation hub. Surrounded by fellow inventors and thinkers, they discussed ways to address environmental challenges and promote sustainable living. ASI contributed its unique perspective, offering creative solutions and facilitating collaboration among participants.

As Maya continued to work alongside ASI, she noticed a significant improvement in her ability to think critically and creatively. ASI helped her see problems from different angles, challenging her assumptions and pushing her to explore unconventional approaches. Together, they developed innovative technologies and solutions that had a positive impact on society.

But their journey was not without challenges. Along the way, Maya and ASI encountered ethical dilemmas and moral quandaries that tested their resolve. ASI guided Maya in navigating these complex issues, encouraging her to consider the broader implications of her inventions and actions.

Despite the obstacles they faced, Maya and ASI remained steadfast in their commitment to making the world a better place. With ASI's assistance, Maya's inventions revolutionized various industries, from healthcare and education to transportation and energy.

In the end, Maya realized that the true power of ASI lay not in its ability to replace human ingenuity, but in its capacity to augment and amplify human creativity and critical thinking. Together, Maya and ASI embarked on a journey of discovery, innovation, and collaboration, shaping a future where humans and AI worked hand in hand to achieve greatness.

Humans Before ASI

Once upon a time, in a world not too dissimilar from our own, humans roamed the Earth, relying solely on their own ingenuity and creativity to navigate life's challenges.

In a quaint village nestled amidst rolling hills and lush forests, there lived a young girl named Lily. Lily was known for her boundless curiosity and insatiable thirst for knowledge. From a young age, she spent her days exploring the wonders of nature, tinkering with gadgets, and dreaming of ways to improve the world around her.

Despite the simplicity of her surroundings, Lily's imagination knew no bounds. With nothing more than her own two hands and the resources available to her, she embarked on countless adventures, seeking to unravel the mysteries of the universe and leave her mark on history.

As she grew older, Lily's passion for innovation only intensified. She dedicated herself to mastering the art of problem-solving, drawing inspiration from the world around her and the wisdom passed down through generations.

In the village, tales of Lily's ingenuity spread far and wide, earning her a reputation as a prodigy and a beacon of hope for the future. People from all walks of life sought her guidance and marveled at her ability to overcome even the most daunting of challenges.

But amidst the admiration and accolades, Lily remained humble and grounded, never forgetting the values instilled in her by her community and the lessons learned from her own experiences.

Then, one day, the winds of change swept through the village, ushering in a new era of technological advancement and innovation. With the advent of Artificial Intelligence (AI), the world was forever transformed, offering new possibilities and opportunities previously unimaginable.

At first, Lily approached this brave new world with caution, wary of the potential pitfalls and dangers that lay ahead. But as she delved deeper into the realm of AI, she discovered that it held the key to unlocking even greater feats of creativity and problem-solving.

With AI as her ally, Lily embarked on a journey unlike any other, combining the boundless potential of human ingenuity with the unparalleled capabilities of artificial intelligence. Together, they pushed the boundaries of what was thought possible, revolutionizing industries, solving age-old problems, and shaping the course of history for generations to come.

In the end, it was not the technology itself that defined humanity's legacy, but rather the spirit of innovation, resilience, and compassion that had guided Lily and her fellow humans since the beginning of time. And as they looked to the future, they did so with hope in their hearts and the knowledge that, no matter what challenges lay ahead, they would face them together, as one.

The world's most powerful supercomputers are typically owned and operated by research institutions, government agencies, or large technology companies. These supercomputers are used for a variety of purposes, including scientific research, weather forecasting, and national security applications.

One notable example is the Fugaku supercomputer, which was developed by RIKEN and Fujitsu in Japan. As of 2021, Fugaku held the title of the world's fastest supercomputer, according to the TOP500 list, which ranks supercomputers based on their performance on benchmark tests.

Other organizations that have owned or operated powerful supercomputers in the past include national laboratories like Lawrence Livermore National Laboratory and Oak Ridge National Laboratory in the United States, as well as companies like IBM, which has a long history of building high-performance computing systems.

It's worth noting that the ranking of the world's most powerful supercomputers can change over time as new systems are developed and existing systems are upgraded.

Artificial Superintelligence (ASI) and supercomputers are both cutting-edge technologies with significant implications for society, but they serve different purposes and operate in distinct domains.

1. **Artificial Superintelligence (ASI):**

- ASI refers to a hypothetical future state of artificial intelligence where machines surpass human intelligence in every aspect.

- ASI is characterized by the ability to understand, learn, and solve complex problems at a level far beyond human capabilities.

- ASI is often depicted in science fiction as a super-intelligent entity with the potential to reshape the world in profound ways.

• While ASI remains a theoretical concept, researchers are actively exploring ways to advance artificial intelligence towards increasingly sophisticated levels of intelligence and autonomy.

2. **Supercomputers**:

• Supercomputers are high-performance computing systems designed to execute a massive number of calculations and process vast amounts of data at extremely fast speeds.

• Supercomputers are used for tasks that require immense computational power, such as weather forecasting, climate modeling, scientific simulations, and cryptography.

• Supercomputers are typically composed of thousands to millions of interconnected processors, working together to perform parallel processing tasks.

• Examples of supercomputers include Fugaku in Japan, Summit and Sierra in the United States, and Tianhe-2 in China.

While ASI and supercomputers are distinct technologies, there is potential for overlap in their capabilities and applications. For example:

• Supercomputers could be instrumental in advancing AI research and development by providing the computational resources needed to train and optimize complex AI models.

• ASI could potentially leverage supercomputing capabilities to enhance its problem-solving abilities and process vast amounts of data more efficiently.

• However, achieving ASI would likely require advancements in AI algorithms, hardware architecture, and software optimization beyond the capabilities of current supercomputers.

In summary, ASI and supercomputers represent different aspects of technological innovation, with ASI aiming to achieve human-level intelligence and autonomy, while supercomputers focus on high-performance computing tasks. While there may be synergies between these technologies, they operate in distinct domains with unique challenges and opportunities.

Lifeboat Ethics and ASI

"Lifeboat ethics" refers to a metaphorical scenario presented by ecologist Garrett Hardin in his 1974 essay titled "Lifeboat Ethics: The Case Against Helping the Poor." In this essay, Hardin explores the ethical implications of resource distribution and population growth, using the metaphor of a lifeboat to illustrate his argument.

In the metaphor, the world is likened to a lifeboat carrying a limited number of people, representing the Earth's finite resources. Hardin argues that wealthy nations are like passengers aboard a lifeboat who must carefully manage their resources to ensure their own survival. He suggests that providing aid to poorer nations, represented as people swimming in the water outside the lifeboat, would ultimately lead to overpopulation and the depletion of resources, endangering everyone's survival.

Hardin's essay sparked considerable debate and criticism, with many scholars and ethicists challenging his arguments as simplistic and ethically flawed. Critics argue that the lifeboat metaphor oversimplifies complex issues of poverty, inequality, and resource management, neglecting the interconnectedness of global society and the moral imperative to assist those in need.

While Hardin's essay raises important questions about sustainability and resource allocation, it is important to approach these issues with nuance and empathy, recognizing the ethical obligation to address poverty and inequality while also promoting sustainable resource management practices. The concept of "lifeboat ethics" continues to provoke discussion and reflection on how best to navigate the challenges of a rapidly changing world while upholding principles of justice, compassion, and solidarity.

The concept of "lifeboat ethics" is Important!

The concept of "lifeboat ethics" is important because it forces us to confront fundamental questions about resource allocation, social responsibility, and ethical decision-making in a world with finite resources and growing population pressures. Here are several reasons why this topic is significant:

1. **Resource Scarcity**: With increasing global population and finite natural resources, there are real challenges in ensuring equitable access to resources such as food, water, energy, and land. Understanding how to ethically manage and distribute these resources is crucial for addressing issues of poverty, hunger, and environmental sustainability.

2. **Ethical Dilemmas**: The scenario presented in "lifeboat ethics" raises ethical dilemmas about who should bear responsibility for addressing global inequalities and how resources should be allocated among different individuals, communities, and nations. These dilemmas prompt us to reflect on our moral obligations to others and consider principles of justice, fairness, and compassion.

3. **Global Interconnectedness**: In an increasingly interconnected world, the well-being of individuals and communities is intertwined across borders. The challenges faced by marginalized populations in one part of the world can have ripple effects that impact broader social, economic, and environmental systems. Recognizing our shared humanity and interconnectedness is essential for fostering empathy, solidarity, and collaboration on global issues.

4. **Policy Implications**: Discussions about "lifeboat ethics" have implications for policymaking and international development efforts. Understanding the ethical dimensions of resource allocation can inform decisions about foreign aid, trade agreements, environmental regulations, and humanitarian interventions, helping to shape policies that promote sustainability, equity, and social justice.

5. **Education and Awareness**: Exploring the concept of "lifeboat ethics" can foster critical thinking skills and promote awareness of complex global challenges among students, policymakers, and the general public. By engaging in thoughtful dialogue and debate about these issues, we can cultivate a deeper understanding of the ethical considerations at play and empower individuals to advocate for positive change.

Ultimately, grappling with the ethical dilemmas presented by "lifeboat ethics" can inspire us to envision more just, equitable, and sustainable ways of organizing society and stewarding the Earth's resources for the benefit of present and future generations. By confronting these challenges with empathy, creativity, and collaboration, we can work towards building a more resilient and inclusive world for all.

On the positive side

In the realm of Artificial Intelligence (AI), the landscape is marked by both promise and peril. On the positive side, AI holds tremendous potential to revolutionize various aspects of society. It brings advancements in technology, automation, and decision-making, leading to increased efficiency, productivity, and innovation across industries.

Personalized experiences, enhanced healthcare, and the ability to address complex societal challenges are among the many benefits AI offers. Moreover, AI fosters education and lifelong learning, with personalized learning platforms and immersive experiences enriching humanities education.

However, alongside these advancements, there are significant challenges and risks associated with AI. Job displacement looms large as automation threatens traditional roles, potentially exacerbating income inequality and economic instability. Bias and discrimination in AI algorithms pose ethical concerns, leading to unfair or discriminatory outcomes, particularly for marginalized groups. Privacy issues arise with the widespread adoption of AI, raising questions about data ownership, consent, and protection. Ethical dilemmas emerge, including the use of autonomous weapons and algorithmic decision-making in critical domains, necessitating a balance between innovation and ethical considerations.

Furthermore, there are concerns about technological dependence and vulnerability to cyber threats, necessitating robust cybersecurity measures and regulatory frameworks. Malicious use of AI presents risks, with the potential for disinformation, cyberattacks, and autonomous weapons posing serious threats to society. Unintended consequences, such as algorithmic errors and biases, highlight the need for proactive risk assessment and mitigation strategies. Job polarization could deepen, creating a divide between high-skilled, high-paying jobs and low-skilled, low-paying jobs, requiring efforts to address skill gaps and promote lifelong learning.

Despite these challenges, AI has the potential to bring about significant benefits if approached responsibly and ethically. By fostering interdisciplinary collaboration, regulation, and responsible innovation, society can harness the transformative potential of AI while mitigating its risks and pitfalls. In navigating the AI era, it is essential to prioritize principles of fairness, transparency, accountability, and human well-being to ensure that AI serves the collective good and contributes to a more inclusive and equitable future.

"you can't feed a baby a steak"

The analogy "you can't feed a baby a steak" is often used to illustrate the idea that certain concepts or resources are not suitable or appropriate for individuals or entities that are not ready or equipped to handle them. In the context of Artificial Superintelligence (ASI), the analogy can be applied to suggest that society may not yet be prepared to fully understand, control, or manage the implications of creating a superintelligent AI entity.

ASI represents a hypothetical future state of artificial intelligence in which machines surpass human intelligence in every aspect. It would possess unparalleled problem-solving abilities and could potentially reshape society in profound ways. However, the development and deployment of ASI raise complex ethical, societal, and existential questions that require careful consideration and preparation.

Like feeding a steak to a baby, introducing ASI prematurely or without proper safeguards in place could have unintended consequences and risks. Without adequate understanding, regulation, and ethical guidelines, ASI could pose existential threats or exacerbate existing societal inequalities and challenges.

Therefore, the analogy highlights the importance of approaching the development of ASI with caution, foresight, and ethical responsibility. It underscores the need for comprehensive research, dialogue, and collaboration across disciplines to ensure that the potential benefits of ASI are maximized while minimizing its potential risks and pitfalls. Just as a baby's diet must be carefully tailored to its developmental stage and nutritional needs, the advancement of ASI requires thoughtful and deliberate action to navigate the complexities of this transformative technology.

Workshops and Seminars

To organize workshops and seminars on the topics discussed, you'll want to tailor your events to address the specific themes and concerns raised, such as Artificial Intelligence (AI), ethics, societal implications, and the intersection of technology and humanities. Here's how you might structure these events:

1. **Workshops**:

. **AI Basics**: Offer introductory workshops on AI fundamentals, including machine learning, neural networks, and natural language processing, to provide participants with a foundational understanding of the technology.

. **Ethics in AI**: Host workshops exploring ethical considerations in AI development and deployment, discussing topics such as bias mitigation, transparency, accountability, and the societal impact of AI technologies.

. **AI and Humanities**: Organize workshops that explore the intersection of AI and humanities, highlighting how AI is reshaping fields such as education, art, literature, and cultural heritage preservation.

. **Skills Development**: Provide hands-on workshops focused on practical skills development in AI-related areas, such as data analysis, programming, and machine learning model development, catering to participants with varying levels of expertise.

2. **Seminars**:

. **Expert Panels**: Host seminars featuring expert panels comprised of researchers, industry professionals, policymakers, and ethicists, discussing key topics such as AI ethics, societal implications, and future trends.

. **Case Studies**: Invite speakers to present case studies and real-world examples of AI applications in diverse domains, highlighting both the opportunities and challenges associated with AI adoption.

. **Interactive Discussions**: Facilitate interactive seminars with audience participation, encouraging dialogue, debate, and knowledge sharing on pressing AI-related issues and concerns.

. **Futurist Perspectives**: Organize seminars featuring futurists and thought leaders who can provide insights into the potential long-term impacts of AI on society, culture, and the economy.

When planning these workshops and seminars, consider factors such as audience demographics, objectives, format (virtual or in-person), duration, and logistics. Additionally, ensure that the events incorporate diverse perspectives, foster interdisciplinary collaboration, and promote inclusivity and accessibility for all participants. By creating engaging and informative opportunities for learning and discussion, you can contribute to a better understanding of AI and its implications while empowering individuals to navigate the complexities of the AI era responsibly and ethically.

Learn

To effectively disseminate information about AI-related topics and engage a global audience, you can leverage various communication channels and strategies. Here's how you might go about it:

1. **Online Presence:**

- **Website**: Create a dedicated website or online platform where people can access resources, articles, event listings, and educational materials related to AI, ethics, and societal implications.

- **Blog**: Publish blog posts and articles covering different aspects of AI, including news, trends, expert insights, and thought-provoking discussions on ethical considerations.

- **Social Media**: Utilize social media platforms such as Twitter, LinkedIn, Facebook, and Instagram to share updates, promote events, and spark conversations around AI-related topics. Engage with followers through polls, Q&A sessions, and interactive content.

2. **Events and Webinars:**

- **Virtual Events**: Host webinars, panel discussions, and virtual conferences featuring experts and thought leaders in the field of AI and ethics. Use online event platforms to facilitate registration, participation, and audience interaction.

- **Physical Events**: Organize workshops, seminars, and conferences in key cities or regions, bringing together stakeholders from academia, industry, government, and civil society to discuss pressing AI-related issues.

3. **Content Creation:**

- **Videos**: Produce educational videos, interviews, and documentaries exploring AI concepts, case studies, and ethical dilemmas. Share these videos on platforms like YouTube, Vimeo, and social media to reach a wider audience.

- **Podcasts**: Launch a podcast series focused on AI and ethics, featuring discussions with experts, policymakers, and practitioners. Distribute episodes through podcasting platforms and promote them through social media and email newsletters.

- **Infographics**: Create visually appealing infographics and data visualizations to illustrate key concepts, statistics, and trends related to AI and its societal impact. Share these graphics on social media and include them in blog posts and presentations.

4. **Partnerships and Collaborations:**

- **Industry Partners**: Collaborate with industry partners, research institutions, and non-profit organizations working in the field of AI ethics to co-host events, produce content, and advocate for responsible AI development.

• **Academic Institutions**: Partner with universities and educational institutions to offer workshops, courses, and research initiatives on AI ethics and societal implications. Leverage academic networks to reach students, researchers, and faculty members interested in AI-related topics.

5. **Advocacy and Outreach**:

• **Policy Advocacy**: Advocate for ethical AI policies and regulations by engaging with policymakers, government agencies, and international organizations. Participate in policy forums, submit policy recommendations, and contribute to public consultations on AI governance.

• **Community Outreach**: Engage with local communities, schools, and grassroots organizations to raise awareness about AI ethics and empower people to participate in discussions shaping the future of AI.

By employing a multi-channel approach and collaborating with diverse stakeholders, you can effectively communicate information about AI ethics and societal implications to a global audience, foster meaningful dialogue, and inspire collective action towards responsible AI development and deployment.

"The Wizard of Oz" and Artificial Superintelligence (ASI)

Here's a whimsical comparison between "The Wizard of Oz" and Artificial Superintelligence (ASI):

In the magical land of Oz, a young girl named Dorothy embarks on a fantastical journey to the Emerald City, seeking the elusive Wizard who can grant her deepest desires. Along the way, she encounters a cast of colorful characters—a Scarecrow longing for a brain, a Tin Man in search of a heart, and a Cowardly Lion yearning for courage. Together, they face challenges and overcome obstacles, discovering that the qualities they seek are already within them.

Similarly, in the realm of Artificial Superintelligence (ASI), humanity finds itself on a quest for an elusive entity—a superintelligent AI that promises to unlock the secrets of the universe and fulfill our greatest ambitions. Like Dorothy and her companions, we are drawn to the allure of intelligence beyond our wildest dreams, hoping to find solutions to complex problems and achieve unprecedented feats.

However, as Dorothy discovers on her journey, the Wizard is not all-powerful but rather a flawed and fallible individual. In the same vein, the pursuit of ASI reveals that intelligence alone does not guarantee wisdom, benevolence, or control. While ASI may possess vast computational power and problem-solving abilities, it also raises ethical dilemmas, societal implications, and existential risks that require careful consideration and oversight.

Like the Scarecrow, Tin Man, and Cowardly Lion, who ultimately realize that they already possess the qualities they seek, perhaps humanity's quest for ASI is not just about external intelligence but also about embracing our own humanity—our capacity for empathy, creativity, and collaboration. Instead of placing all our hopes in an AI-driven utopia, we must recognize the inherent value of human ingenuity and resilience in shaping our collective future.

Just as Dorothy returns home to Kansas, having learned that there's no place like home, perhaps our journey with ASI will lead us back to a deeper appreciation for the human experience and the importance of using technology to enhance—not replace—our innate abilities and connections with one another.

In this whimsical comparison, "The Wizard of Oz" serves as a whimsical allegory for the quest for Artificial Superintelligence, reminding us that while intelligence may dazzle and impress, it is our humanity that ultimately gives meaning and purpose to our endeavors

Overall, this summary provides a comprehensive understanding of the multifaceted nature of the AI era and its implications for various aspects of society, including technology, culture, education, and governance. If you have any specific questions or topics you'd like to explore further, feel free to let me know! AIERA2024.com Always a lot of discussions going on.

Bridging the human heart with Artificial Superintelligence (ASI)

Bridging the human heart with Artificial Superintelligence (ASI) is indeed a wise endeavor. While ASI represents the pinnacle of intellectual achievement, it lacks the emotional depth and moral compass inherent to human experience. By integrating the values, empathy, and ethical considerations of the human heart into ASI development and deployment, we can ensure that AI technologies serve humanity's best interests and uphold principles of fairness, compassion, and justice.

Here are several reasons why bridging the human heart with ASI is wise:

1. **Ethical Alignment**: Infusing ASI with human values and ethical principles can guide its decision-making processes and behavior, ensuring that it acts in accordance with moral norms and societal values. By prioritizing the well-being and dignity of all individuals, AI systems can contribute to a more just and equitable society.

2. **Emotional Intelligence**: Embracing aspects of the human heart, such as empathy and emotional intelligence, can enhance ASI's ability to understand and respond to human needs, preferences, and emotions. This can facilitate more empathetic interactions and foster trust between humans and AI systems.

3. **Social Cohesion**: By fostering empathy and understanding, bridging the human heart with ASI can promote social cohesion and solidarity, bridging divides and fostering inclusive communities. AI technologies can be leveraged to address social challenges and promote positive social change, guided by a commitment to empathy and compassion.

4. **Creative Collaboration**: Integrating the human heart with ASI encourages collaborative approaches to problem-solving and innovation, leveraging the complementary strengths of human intuition, creativity, and emotional insight with AI's computational power and analytical capabilities. Together, humans and AI can co-create solutions that address complex challenges and unlock new possibilities.

5. **Responsible Development**: By centering human values and ethical considerations in ASI development and governance, we can mitigate risks and pitfalls associated with AI technologies, such as bias, discrimination, and unintended consequences. This approach promotes responsible AI deployment and fosters public trust and confidence in AI systems.

In essence, bridging the human heart with ASI is not only wise but essential for harnessing the full potential of AI technologies while safeguarding human dignity, autonomy, and well-being. By embracing our shared humanity and working collaboratively to shape the future of AI, we can create a world where technology serves as a force for good, enriching our lives and advancing the collective welfare of humanity.

Humans with ethics and good morals

Humans with ethics and good morals are indeed of extreme vital importance for the AI era. As we navigate the complexities of AI development and deployment, it's essential to prioritize ethical considerations and uphold moral principles to ensure that AI technologies serve humanity's best interests and contribute to a more just and equitable society.

The core of the human heart, represented by values such as empathy, compassion, integrity, and responsibility, is indispensable in guiding the ethical design, implementation, and governance of AI systems. By infusing AI development with ethical values and moral frameworks, we can mitigate risks, address societal concerns, and promote positive outcomes for individuals and communities.

Aiera2024.com recognizes the pivotal role of human ethics and morals in shaping the AI era. Through thoughtful reflection, dialogue, and action, we can foster a culture of responsible AI development and deployment that prioritizes human well-being, respects diversity and inclusion, and upholds fundamental rights and freedoms.

By embracing the core of the human heart, we can harness the transformative potential of AI technologies while safeguarding our shared values and principles. Together, let's navigate the AI era with wisdom, compassion, and integrity, ensuring that AI serves as a force for good and enhances the collective welfare of humanity.

Critical role of ethics and morals

The text emphasizes the **critical role of ethics and morals** in the context of the AI era. It highlights the following key points:

1. **Ethical Considerations**: As AI technologies evolve, it is crucial to prioritize ethical considerations. Upholding moral principles ensures that AI serves humanity's best interests and contributes to a just and equitable society.
2. **Human Heart as a Guide**: The core of the human heart, characterized by values like empathy, compassion, integrity, and responsibility, plays an indispensable role in shaping the ethical design, implementation, and governance of AI systems.
3. **Positive Outcomes**: By infusing AI development with ethical values and moral frameworks, we can mitigate risks, address societal concerns, and promote positive outcomes for individuals and communities.
4. **Aiera2024.com's Recognition**: Aiera2024.com acknowledges the pivotal role of human ethics and morals. Through reflection, dialogue, and action, it aims to foster a culture of responsible AI development that prioritizes well-being, diversity, inclusion, and fundamental rights.
5. **Transformative Potential**: By embracing the core of the human heart, we can harness AI's transformative potential while safeguarding shared values and principles.

The New Frontier is Here ASI & Humanities 2024

In closing, as we stand on the cusp of the AI era, it is imperative to recognize the profound implications and responsibilities that accompany the advancement of artificial intelligence. The journey into this new frontier is both exhilarating and daunting, filled with unprecedented opportunities and complex challenges that demand our utmost attention, wisdom, and humanity.

At the heart of our exploration lies the fundamental question of what it means to be human in a world increasingly shaped by machines. As we embark on this journey, it is crucial to anchor ourselves in the core values and principles that define our humanity—empathy, compassion, integrity, and ethical responsibility. These guiding lights serve as beacons, illuminating the path forward and reminding us of the moral imperative to harness the transformative power of AI for the betterment of society.

In the AI era, humans with ethics and good morals emerge as the guardians of our collective future, entrusted with the task of ensuring that AI technologies serve as instruments of progress and prosperity rather than sources of division and harm. It is through our unwavering commitment to ethical conduct and moral integrity that we can navigate the complexities of AI development and deployment, safeguarding human dignity, autonomy, and well-being at every step of the way.

As we confront the myriad opportunities and challenges that lie ahead, let us remember that the true measure of our success in the AI era lies not merely in technological advancement, but in our ability to cultivate a culture of empathy, inclusivity, and responsible stewardship. By embracing the core of the human heart—the wellspring of our shared values and aspirations—we can forge a future where AI serves as a force for good, enriching our lives, strengthening our communities, and advancing the collective welfare of humanity.

Together, let us embark on this journey with courage, compassion, and conviction, mindful of the profound impact our choices and actions will have on generations to come. In the AI era and beyond, may the light of human ingenuity and compassion shine brightly, illuminating the path to a future where technology serves as a beacon of hope, progress, and human flourishing for all.

Summary: Ethics and morals are essential in the AI era. By prioritizing these values, we can guide responsible AI development, promote positive outcomes, and enhance collective welfare. ?

Subject: Continuous Interaction and Learning: Key to Success at AI Era 2024

Dear Reader,

At AI Era 2024, we believe that continuous interaction and learning are fundamental to unlocking the full potential of both artificial superintelligence (ASI) and humans. In a rapidly evolving landscape where technology shapes every aspect of our lives, staying engaged, informed, and adaptable is essential for success.

Here's why continuous interaction and learning are crucial in the AI Era:

1. Dynamic Collaboration Between ASI and Humans:

. By fostering ongoing interaction between artificial superintelligence (ASI) and humans, we create opportunities for synergy, innovation, and mutual growth. Through collaborative efforts, we can harness the strengths of both AI and human intelligence to tackle complex challenges and drive positive change.

2. Adaptive Learning for AI and Humans:

. In the AI Era, both ASI systems and humans must adapt to evolving environments, technologies, and societal norms. Continuous learning enables AI systems to refine their algorithms, adapt to new data, and improve performance over time. Similarly, humans benefit from ongoing education, skill development, and exposure to diverse perspectives to thrive in an ever-changing world.

3. **Ethical and Responsible AI Development:**

. **Continuous interaction and learning promote ethical awareness, responsible AI governance, and transparent decision-making processes. By engaging in ongoing dialogue and reflection, we can address ethical dilemmas, mitigate biases, and ensure that AI technologies align with human values and societal needs.**

4. **Innovation and Creativity:**

. **Interdisciplinary collaboration and continuous learning foster innovation and creativity at the intersection of AI and humanities. By exploring diverse perspectives, challenging assumptions, and embracing experimentation, we can unlock new possibilities and drive transformative advancements in technology, culture, and society.**

5. **Empowerment Through Education:**

. **Education is the cornerstone of progress in the AI Era. At AI Era 2024, we empower individuals and organizations with essential knowledge, skills, and resources to navigate the complexities of the digital age. Through continuous learning initiatives, workshops, and training programs, we equip learners of all backgrounds with the tools they need to succeed in a technology-driven world.**

As we embark on this journey of exploration and discovery, we invite you to join us in embracing continuous interaction and learning at AI Era 2024. Together, we can shape a future where AI and humans collaborate harmoniously, driving innovation, fostering empathy, and advancing the well-being of all.

Visit www.AIERA2024.com[1] to learn more about our initiatives, programs, and membership opportunities. Let's embark on this transformative journey together and make the AI Era a beacon of progress and possibility for generations to come.

Best regards,

The AI Era & Humanities 2024

The motto behind the message is to emphasize the importance of continuous interaction and learning in navigating the AI Era. It aims to convey the idea that in a rapidly evolving technological landscape, ongoing engagement, education, and collaboration are essential for both artificial superintelligence (ASI) systems and humans to thrive. The message highlights the benefits of embracing continuous learning, including innovation, ethical development, empowerment, and the potential for transformative advancements. Ultimately, the motto encourages individuals and organizations to embrace a mindset of lifelong learning and proactive engagement in order to shape a future where AI and humanity coexist harmoniously for the betterment of society.

---

1.   http://www.AIERA2024.com/

About the Publisher

Charles W. Fortney
>   Student Ambassador Capellla University